Three Rivers Crossing

Robert A. Lytle

To Norman Bud Hughes
Best Wishes
Robert A Lytle
_3-21-00_

River Road Publications, Inc.

Spring Lake, Michigan

Hardcover ISBN: 0-938682-55-5
Paperback ISBN: 0-938682-60-1
Printed in the United States of America

✍ *Dedication* ☞

This story is dedicated to our pioneer ancestors who left their homes in New England for the chance to better their lives on the Great Lakes frontier. Hundreds of tiny villages, such as Stony Creek, Michigan, were settled in a manner similar to that described within the chapters of this story. Each settlement had its own set of characters and tales. Your local library or historical society will help you discover the adventures the founders of your town encountered in its settling stages. With their help and your imagination, you may write your own version of *Three Rivers Crossing*.

Twenty-five years ago I spent many months with my father helping him record the memories of his youth. His purpose was to ensure that his grandchildren would know what it was like to live as he did on a Michigan farm at the turn of the twentieth century. Although I was a city-boy, it was my job to make his farm-boy stories understandable to those from other generations and lifestyles. Working with my father during those three years—he was in his seventies and I was in my thirties—I came to understand him as I never had before. That we waited until so late in his life to begin this project is regrettable. He died only a week after *The Lytles—Their Life on the Farm* was published in 1977, one of the proudest days in each of our lives. It is for him, Howard Harold Lytle, that I dedicate this book.

❧ *Contents* ❧

Chapter 1	Three Rivers Crossing	1
Chapter 2	The Trout Stream	12
Chapter 3	An Ancient Link	18
Chapter 4	The Truth	25
Chapter 5	Tales	34
Chapter 6	The Test	40
Chapter 7	Rodeo Rider	47
Chapter 8	First Evening	51
Chapter 9	Night Thoughts	56
Chapter 10	Rochester	63
Chapter 11	The Mail	71
Chapter 12	Home	76
Chapter 13	The Encounter	82
Chapter 14	June	88
Chapter 15	Grayling	93
Chapter 16	Governor Cass	100
Chapter 17	The Future	106
Chapter 18	Planting	114
Chapter 19	Lemuel's Decision	122
Chapter 20	The Mill	127
Chapter 21	Return	136
Chapter 22	The Letter	145
Chapter 23	The Promise	156

❧ *A Special Thanks* ☙

No task is as fun as when it can be done with the help of friends. Many contributed their time and talents for this story: Dick and Mary Eberline, Cammie Mannino, Louise Abnee, Nancy Bujold, Bill and Diane Ebinger, Kathy Shellenbarger and her niece, Katie Crane, Ray Lawson, Ken Johnson, George Bowersox, and Brian Seyburn. Mrs. Brook Qualman's entire fourth grade class at Hampton Elementary School read and reviewed at least one of the drafts, commenting and suggesting changes. The result, hopefully, is that this story will be as much fun to read as it was to write.

There are others who also need to be mentioned. Terry Upton, Dennis Fogler, Randy Gehrke and members of the Rochester Hills Museum staff, Jill Waldecker and Patricia Brown, contributed with their historical knowledge. Dave Shellenbarger, who has often come to my rescue when my computer has refused to budge beyond a C-prompt, assisted with many valuable suggestions for the story line. Finally, but certainly not least, is my wife Candy, whose support has been instrumental thoroughout all of my writing endeavors. My appreciation goes out to all of you.

Introduction

By defeating the British in the War of 1812, the United States of America won title to an area of land that substantially increased its previous boundaries. U.S. political leaders were anxious to have this newly acquired region settled by loyal Americans. To do this they offered large plats of land at low prices on the Great Lakes frontier.

The pioneer families who came found a hostile environment. Native American Indians who had fought for the British tested even the sturdiest pioneer. Most of Michigan Territory's tillable farmland was guarded by miles of impassable swamps or impenetrable forests. Added to that were the ever-present foes of famine, plague, and pestilence. These were barriers and terrifying situations for which the East coast farmers were unprepared.

Still, our forefathers survived and even thrived. Each person, regardless of age or social status, became a valuable asset to the fragile balance of the community. Indeed, each child's birth was a blessing. Each was a hope for the future. At the same time a citizen's death brought not only sadness, but a hardship upon the village. That person's duties would need to be assumed by already overburdened citizens.

Some of those early settlements grew and prospered into our present villages and cities. Many towns, often with charming names such as Hog's Hollow and Rudd's Mill, withered and died. A precious few, such as the town in the following story, Stony Creek, is a treasure from the past. It has remained almost unchanged from its frontier beginnings.

Chapter 1

❦ *Three Rivers Crossing* ❦

Walker Morrison stared through the open school window watching a cardinal flit from one maple branch to another. Sitting through the last hour on a warm Friday in late May was pure agony. Visions of fat rainbow trout prowling the deep, blue pools of Stony Creek stole Walker's attention from the history lecture Mr. McKay was giving to his seventh grade class.

"In the spring of 1823," Mr. McKay said, standing at the blackboard, "Lemuel Taylor led his family and friends, sixty people in all, from the safety of their homes in New York State to the unknown dangers of Michigan Territory."

Mr. McKay was the guest teacher for Mr. Dillon's class that day. He was in charge of the Rochester Hills Museum at VanHoosen Farm in nearby Stony Creek. He was often asked to speak when any Rochester school was studying local history. He could make Michigan's past jump to life for his listeners–normally. But the perfect weather outdoors combined with the lateness of the school day indoors was more than this seventh grade class could bear.

Still, Mr. McKay continued. "The Taylors struggled through long, cold days on overland trails, canals, rivers, and lakes. Their last rest stop was at Rochester, Michigan Territory, a tiny new settlement known by the local Ojibwa Indians as 'Three Rivers Crossing.'"

Mr. McKay unfolded a stiff parchment map of Michigan Territory which the Taylor family had used on their journey almost two centuries before. It didn't look at all like the modern map hanging on the wall a few feet away. This one seemed more as if a glacier had rolled over the Great Lakes sometime between 1820 and 2002, changing the entire shape of the state. Mr. McKay pointed to a spot where three curly lines joined together and led eastward to Lake Saint Clair.

"On the morning of May 15, 1823, the Taylors left Rochester and walked the final mile-and-a-quarter to the site of their new settlement which they called Stony Creek Village."

As the second hand on the classroom clock moved up to the last twenty seconds of the 3:15 mark, Walker and the other students began to gather their books.

"I see a familiar name on Mr. Dillon's class roll," Mr. McKay said. "I have to ask. Walker Morrison, are you here?"

"Y'sir," Walker said from the back of the room.

"Do you know if you are related to the Stony Creek Taylors?" Mr. McKay said. He sounded almost hopeful that the answer would be no.

2

"Way back," Walker said. "My dad's great-great-grandmother, or something like that, was a Taylor. Eunice was her name."

A stunned expression crossed Mr. McKay's face.

The bell rang, and class was over. Walker turned his attention to hurrying home, gathering his fishing gear, and getting out on the river. Laws should protect kids from having to listen to boring history lessons on days like this, he thought.

Besides, he'd heard the story about the Taylor family coming to Michigan about a hundred times from his dad. It wasn't as if he didn't care–they were his own ancestors. But if he couldn't get into this history stuff, how could they expect anyone else to, least of all his Hart Middle classmates. Most of them weren't even from around here.

Hart was set square in the middle of one of the most upwardly mobile towns in America. To Walker, "upwardly" meant that many of these kids' parents were rich. "Mobile" meant that they came and went like so many monarch butterflies. Moving vans and "For Sale" signs were as common as BMW, Jaguar, and Mercedes Benz cars. Many of the parents were auto executives who were constantly being shuffled from one car-making city to another. For them, Rochester was nothing more than a pit stop between exciting places in Germany, France, Japan, or England. These jet-set kids wouldn't give a rip about how Lemuel Taylor brought his family from New York to Stony Creek in 1823.

Plus, what Mr. McKay was talking about had happened ages ago. Walker knew one thing for sure—studying anything that old was just plain dull. It might be okay if history actually repeated itself like he'd heard people say. That would be cool. But it never did. Not exactly, anyway. So what good was it to learn all those old names and dates? If there was a course about the future, well, that would be something he could really get into.

Walker slowly uncorked himself from his chair. He was already six foot, two inches tall and as a seventh grader, had outgrown all the desks at Hart. He still had a year to go before entering Rochester High and getting some decent-sized furniture.

He sometimes awakened at night from a dream where he was sitting in school and had grown so much during one class hour that a rescue truck had to come— sirens blaring and red lights flashing—and Chief Gray would have to pry him out of his desk with the Jaws of Life.

Walker stretched his muscles and stood a full head taller than most of his classmates. He glanced up and saw, coming in his direction, the one girl he completely fell apart over. Renee St. Jean had transferred in from Paris, France, in January. Her gorgeous face, fabulous body, and beguiling mannerisms had captured the attention of every boy at Hart Middle School from her very first day.

The feeling, evidently, was not mutual. Renee was as aloof in her regard for the Hart boys as she was enchanting to them. Walker's mother told him that Renee was probably just shy, and that once she became comfortable with her new surroundings she would be just like everyone else. Walker didn't buy that for a second. Renee was so far above the Hart kids that he couldn't believe she would ever notice any of them, much less actually speak to them.

Walker froze next to Mr. Dillon's desk as Renee moved gracefully down the aisle. Her gaze was fixed squarely on Walker's face. Walker's knees buckled, and he jammed his knuckles into a pile of term papers that Mr. Dillon was about to take home.

Renee's eyes were soft brown, as was her long, wavy hair. But it was her stunning face that seized Walker's soul. Her lips were moving as she approached, but Walker's brain was overcome by an avalanche of stimuli. He hadn't heard a word she'd said.

Finally, Walker glanced to each side and then pointed a finger to his chest. "You talking to me?" he blurted out.

"*Mais oui*," she said. She put her hand to her mouth and smiled. "Pardon me," she said, "your name eez Wokair, no?"

"Uh, yeah," Walker said, still holding himself up with his knuckles which were tingling now from lack of circulation.

"Oh, good. It eez that you remind me so much of a boy at my school in Paree that I think you must also speak my language. Do you speak French, Wokair?"

Walker shook his head. She pronounced his name like no one else ever had. Suddenly, the old way of saying Walker seemed dull, and he didn't care if the other guys made fun of it, which he was sure they would. "Wok-AIR," he could already hear them say. Well, they could just stick their heads in the john and flush themselves all the way to Lake Saint Clair.

"Eez it true that you are related to the settlers of this cute little town where I live?" she asked, singing to him with her melodious French accent. "It eez as if you are a part of your country's history, no?"

"Y-you live out by Stony Creek?" Walker croaked. Compared to hers, his voice sounded like a banjo bashing about in a Brahms' lullaby.

"Yes," she said. "My family lives at the end of Stony Pointe overlooking VanHoosen Farm. It eez beautiful there, no? It eez like Loire Valley where my father keeps a small chalet. We visit there every summer."

Walker's throat was dry. His voice had become an unintelligible gurgle. It was just as well because he couldn't think of a thing to say—certainly nothing he wouldn't immediately regret. There was a long, awkward moment in which Walker was supposed to reply. He did not, could not, respond. Instead he stared dumbly into her eyes.

"Good-bye, Wokair," she said and began to turn away. Walker tried frantically to think of something that would continue the conversation, but he was completely tongue-tied. Renee stepped around Mr. McKay who was staring at Walker with an expression of wonder. Walker looked past him as Renee moved through the classroom door. The moment she stepped into the hallway, his brain snapped out of its vapor lock.

An entire conversation leaped into Walker's head. *So nice to talk to you, Renee. Perhaps we might study together soon. We could discuss this area's early history. My family is one of the first in Oakland County. Yes, I visit Stony Creek often, and it certainly reminds me of the Loire Valley, too. As it happens, I am going there this afternoon. No, no, not the Loire Valley, ha, ha, I mean Stony Creek. You see, I am an experienced fly-fisherman. Stony Creek is one of my favorite streams. Perhaps I could show you how it is done, yes? I am certain you would enjoy communing with nature as I do.*

Blood returned to Walker's legs and fingers with a painful tingle. He tried to catch her, but by the time he reached the door, she had melted into the molten mass of teenage humanity moving through the halls.

How it was that death was not an hourly occurrence in the seven minutes of mayhem between classes was still a mystery to Walker. Last year, on his first day as a sixth grader, he was thrust into the overcrowded school and was quickly made to realize, especially by the eighth grade boys, that he was the lowest, least important piece of protoplasm on the planet.

Now he was nearly at the end of the seventh grade. He had grown about a foot, earned a letter in swimming and football, and made his mark, at least with the kids at Hart.

Walker hurried to his locker and jammed his history book into a small gap near the top of the tiny compartment. He yanked out his green, nylon jacket with the big, white "H" as he held the rest of the clutter in place with his right knee. Next he grabbed his book bag, spun the dial as the door slapped shut, and forced his way back into the flow of the crowd.

The hall was always noisy, but after the last class on Fridays it was louder than a Mars mission blast-off.

"Hey, Wok-AIR!" a high-pitched voice called from behind.

Walker's heart leaped into his throat. He turned looking for the beautiful face and long brown hair of his gorgeous new friend. Instead, he saw the red hair and freckled forehead of his best buddy, Kenny Fisher, who was waving to him from about ten feet away. Not already, Walker thought. How could he have found out so soon? Kenny's not even in my Michigan history class.

Kenny's smiling eyes were bobbing over the heads of the taller eighth-graders. "Wait up, mon-sewer," he yelled with a fake French accent.

Walker worked his way to the side where the current was not as strong as in midstream.

"What's up, Shrimp?" Walker said, trying to retaliate for his friend's taunt.

"How could she fall for a long, gangly dweeb like you when she's got a really cool guy like me right at her own eye level? Brains and beauty must not cohabit Renee's gene pool," Kenny said. "But, look, we're getting up a volleyball game at the park. I've asked her to join us. How 'bout it?"

"Naw, I'm going fishing," Walker said, shaking his head.

"What if she comes?" Kenny said with a little smile. "If you're not there to show off your primitive, animal-like athletic skills, I might win her over with my sparkling wit, good looks, and magnetic charm. Hey, don't laugh. It could happen."

"Renee would no more play volleyball with you guys in a sand pit than she would swim with the blood suckers at the city pond," Walker said. "Look, I hear the rainbows are hitting at Stony Creek by the old farm museum. If you want to come, fine. Otherwise, I'll see you around." Walker turned toward the door.

"Okay," Kenny said, "but don't say I didn't give you a chance. You'll be sorry when I'm taking Renee to the last school dance next week. Then, of course, she'll be mine for the rest of the summer."

"Right," Walker said. He pushed the door open and

went to the bike stand. Pulling the key from around his neck, he undid the lock and swung the book bag over his shoulder. He pedaled away from school to his house on Fourth Street.

- - - - -

Walker set his kickstand and ran up the front porch stairs of the old, two-story, white frame house. It had been in his family for generations. How many, he didn't know.

"Hi, Mom, I'm home," he yelled.

"How was school?" his mother called back. Walker looked toward the kitchen and saw that she was watching a *Seinfeld* rerun as she ironed her way through a huge pile of laundry.

"Fine. I'm going fishing," he said. He dropped his school bag inside and gathered the fishing gear from its place behind the door. Actually, it was his dad's stuff, but Walker knew his father would be working late and wouldn't mind him using it—especially if he brought home a mess of trout. From the hat rack behind the door he grabbed his lucky Detroit Tigers baseball cap to shade his eyes.

"Okay," his mom called out. "Be home by seven for dinner."

Walker turned and hurried down the front porch steps. He hopped on his bike and rode one block to his dad's drugstore on Main Street. He leaned the two-wheeler against the side wall of the old, orange brick building and ran inside. It, too, had been in the family for ages.

"Hi, Dad," Walker said. He was careful to come in the "Out" door so that the bell on the "In" door wouldn't ring, something that always annoyed Gladys, the tobacco cashier. "I'm going fishing," Walker called over to his father. "Can I take a Coke?"

"Sure," Sam Morrison said, barely looking up from his computer screen. There were several customers nearby, anxious to get their medications and none too thrilled by the interruption caused by the boy's entrance. "Where are you going?" Walker's dad asked, his fingers still tapping the keyboard.

"Stony Creek by the museum."

"Water's pretty high right now, Walker," Mr. Morrison said. He turned and grabbed a small pill bottle from a shelf behind him. He shook it and handed it to Mary, his assistant. "With yesterday's rain, the current will be stronger than usual."

"I'll be careful," Walker said as he headed out. He pulled the "In" door extra hard as he left. The old brass bell jangled loudly over his head. He shot an impish grin back at Gladys who glowered in his direction as he disappeared down the stairs.

Chapter 2

❧ *The Trout Stream* ❧

Walker slid the Coke can in his jacket pocket and jumped on his bike. He pedaled along Main Street and stopped for the light at University. As he began to cross an old Chevy whizzed through the red light. Walker jerked back on his handlebars to avoid being run over. He looked around hoping a cop would nail the idiot driver, but seeing none, he proceeded up Main and turned right on Romeo. A mile down the road Romeo narrowed to a one-lane gravel path as it crested a hill. It had once gone all the way into the tiny historic village, but was now only a bike trail where a cemetery began.

That must be where Renee lives, Walker thought as he passed a huge house overlooking the stream. I wonder if she's home from school yet. She might be sitting on her back patio sipping an iced tea right now. I hope she sees me fishing and comes down to watch.

As dumb as all the Stony Creek history stuff was, this was still Walker's favorite part of Rochester. It was like falling two centuries into the past, from the ultra modern Michigan of 2002 to the very first settling stage of Michigan Territory. Up to the cemetery, everything along Romeo Street was polished steel, concrete, and new construction. There were apartment buildings and tall churches. New subdivisions had huge expensive homes with yards and gardens trimmed to within an inch of their lives. A weed would have no more chance of popping up here than on the surface of the sun.

Walker steered his bike along the narrow lane leading down the hill to the historic village. He glanced to his right at the cemetery and the grave markers of his Taylor ancestors, the first settlers of Stony Creek. An image of his father decked out in his nineteenth century pioneer clothes flashed through Walker's head. His father stood behind Lemuel Taylor's tall, thin tombstone, explaining to a crowd of people what it was like coming here in 1823. It was a scene that took place every Halloween as part of the museum's "Meet the Stony Creek Ghosts" program. A dozen or so other people, some of them kids, would be spread over the ancient graveyard dressed in old-fashioned clothes waiting to tell about their lives—and deaths—at Stony Creek.

Walker hadn't come to watch it since he was eight or nine, but he couldn't go past without thinking about it. It was meant to be educational, but seeing all those people in strange outfits talking about how they died—man, that was too spooky for words. He'd have nightmares of ghosts wriggling out of the ground like snakes. They would snatch him by the ankles and drag him across the bumpy cemetery grounds to their moldy coffins. Just as his head was about to disappear beneath the cold wet sod, Walker would wake up screaming.

Walker coasted his bike to the bottom of the hill and crossed the rickety Stony Creek bridge. Flowing beneath was a beautiful bubbling brook—a stretch of trout stream any fly-fisherman would kill to have for his very own. Beyond that was Stony Creek Village, the perfectly preserved nineteenth-century farm community that Mr. McKay had been droning on about to Walker's class only an hour before.

Walker leaned his bike against the base of the bridge. Scanning the hill behind him where the new homes sat overlooking the stream, he tried to see if Renee was on her patio. But it was risky to stare, just in case she might see him. Deciding to concentrate on fishing, he gathered his gear and stepped down to the river's edge. He set his creel on the grassy bank and popped open the can of soda.

As he took a big slug of Coke, he noticed that the museum was quiet—no weddings, tours, or family reunions were going on. He had the whole place to himself. And today the weather was so warm no waders were needed. He simply rolled up his pantlegs, kept his tennis shoes on to protect his feet from the sharp stones, and waded into the chilly water.

Walker watched the natural flies that were darting along the surface. He decided he'd use a small green caddis fly—one he had made the week before with pheasant feathers tied to a #15 barbed hook. He picked it off the lamb's wool patch of his fishing vest and lashed it with a fisherman's knot to the thread-like leader.

He yanked several yards of line from the reel and flicked a few false casts back and forth before letting the lure drop into a quiet shady area upstream. The water ran blue and deep, and the fly drifted toward him, bouncing in the swirling current.

Suddenly a streak of silver and black caught Walker's eye. Shooting across the bottom of the creek, an enormous fish broke the surface. It took the bait and exploded three feet into the air, its tall dorsal fin fanning the entire length of its broad back. The torpedo-shaped fish twisted violently to dislodge the hook, but splashed back into the stream with the barb still imbedded in its upper lip.

Oh man, Walker thought. If I can land this baby, whatever it is, we're going to eat good tonight. I hope Renee is watching. She won't forget this anytime soon.

The strange fish splashed from bank to bank. It dove and leapt and took more line from Walker's reel as it darted upstream. Walker wished he'd brought his waders now, because the fish was leading him into a dangerous part of the river. Here the water was deep, the current was fast, and a tree had fallen across the shallow side of the stream. If he followed the shallow route, he would almost certainly get his line snarled on a branch. If he tried to pass around the tree on the deep side, the bank was high and the water over his head. No matter which direction he took, he would be in trouble.

I've got to catch this fish, Walker thought. I could take it up to Renee's house, and she'd be really impressed. If I'm careful, I can work my way around this tree and get back to the shallow part without snarling the line.

Walker stepped to his left pointing his rod clear of the tree. Up ahead he watched the fish take another tail-walk across the surface. Its mouth was open and its long dorsal fin stood high on its back. What kind of fish is this? he wondered. He ducked his head under the last branch. The water was already up to his neck and the current was pushing him backwards into the tree, making it harder to keep his footing. The water shouldn't be this deep, Walker thought.

Suddenly a sharp twig scratched Walker's face. He jerked his head in pain. His blue Detroit Tigers cap flew into the air. That's my Kirk Gibson hat, he realized. I can't lose that! Kirk signed it himself!

Walker lunged for his cap, but it landed behind him on the other side of the fallen tree. As he reached, he slipped into deeper water. He was in over his head. His feet frantically searched for a rock—something to push himself to the surface. In a split second his vest became snarled in a tree limb forcing his head under water.

Walker let go of the fly rod and thrashed his arms to untangle himself from the snare. But it was no use. He was caught like a fly in a spider's web.

He had to get air. Frantically, he scissor-kicked upward, risking gashes as he tried to make his way through the sharp branches. But even that didn't work.

Walker's lungs screamed for air. He couldn't hold out another instant. Turning his face upward, he pushed his mouth as near to the surface as he could. The stream flowed slightly above his outstretched lips.

He closed his eyes and inhaled. But the breath he took was not air. It was black Stony Creek water. He gagged as it filled his lungs. A wave of nausea shot through his belly.

The light in his eyes went out and Walker knew it was forever.

Chapter 3

⚞ *An Ancient Link* ⚟

Walker thrashed face down in the grass, barfing his guts out. Buckets of water exploded from his lungs. Slowly he became aware that someone was pushing on his back. Strong hands were lifting his elbows, drawing air into his lungs. He rolled over and opened his eyes. Sunlight blasted over the shoulders of a bearded man who knelt directly in front of him. Walker writhed in agony.

"He is coming to," a young voice yelled. "He is alive!"

Walker never felt less alive in his life. But somehow, he was alive. The old worn-out football blocking dummies at Hart looked better than he felt.

Walker tried to focus on the bearded man's face. Who is this guy? Walker was sure he'd never seen him before.

Walker rolled his head and noticed that he was surrounded by a dozen people dressed in old-fashioned clothes. Museum workers, he thought as he closed his eyes. How did they get down here so fast? Renee must have been watching from her patio, saw me in trouble, and called the museum for help. She's probably here right now. Walker opened his eyes and looked at all the faces. No, she's not here. I guess I'll just get up, grab my bike, and pedal my butt home. As he leaned on his elbow to push himself upward a rush of dizziness forced him back to the ground.

"It would be best if you remained still, lad," the man said with a firm voice. He looked at the woman standing at his side. "Sally, would you bring a blanket? We must keep this young man warm."

An elderly lady wearing a blue gingham dress, white apron, and a black bonnet turned and hurried up the hill toward a log cabin.

"Reverend Taylor, is he going to live?" a man asked.

"I do not know, Peter," the bearded man said. "That decision rests with the Lord. But while he is here, we will help him any way we can."

Walker coughed again. His lungs were on fire. Between dizzy spells, he rolled his head and glanced at the faces staring down at him. None were familiar.

Where am I? Walker wondered.

It was starting to come back to him—casting his fly line—catching the weird-looking fish—getting caught under water. How did I get out of there? How did I get on this bank?

Walker looked around for the museum farmhouse, the cow barns, the big silos. There was nothing. A few log cabins and some small sheds dotted the landscape, but there were none of the usual Stony Creek buildings. I must have been washed downstream, Walker thought. But how far?

Only the river bank itself appeared the same. Walker was lying in a wide, clover-filled meadow, much like the place he always stretched out on when he took a break from fishing. He would lie there and watch the clouds drift by, absorbing the warmth of the sun and the smell of the ground. He would close his eyes and listen to the birds overhead and the water rushing nearby. But this couldn't be the same meadow. There were no barns or silos.

The old lady in the pioneer clothes hurried from the cabin carrying a blue woolen blanket. She opened it and spread it over him. Walker welcomed the warmth.

Someone should be on a cell phone calling 911, he thought. Nobody seems to understand how bad I need a doctor.

"How do you feel, son?" the man asked.

Walker opened his mouth to tell him, but instead coughed so hard that he thought his lungs would come out.

A little girl came and stood beside the bearded man. "Who is he, Daddy?" she asked. "His clothes are so funny." She, too, was dressed in historic garments. Her face, hands, and bare feet were smudged with dirt as though she had been playing in the mud all day.

"Eunice, you must not be so bold," the lady said.

"Well, they are," insisted the girl.

"There now, Eunice," the man said, "all will be well.

You and Daniel may return to help in Elisha's garden."

As he said this, a boy about twelve years old stepped forward to the girl's side. He stared at Walker for a moment and then took her hand. The two of them followed the other people who also moved away from the stream. Only the bearded man and the old woman stayed with Walker.

"We must find out who he is, Lemuel," the woman said. "His family may live nearby."

The man replied, "He could be with the government surveying crew, Sally. Perhaps he is a messenger or an apprentice."

"That is true," she said. "Still, his clothes seem so strange. His sailcloth shoes with their soft soles would not last long in the forest. They are nearly torn away as it is. See here, Lemuel, look at his breeches. Already they have holes in the knees. His shirt is so thin—and his jacket. Neither has proper sleeves. Whatever could he be doing wearing such flimsy apparel?"

"The rest of the survey crew may be upstream," the bearded man said. "Perhaps he had an accident, Sally. All of his regular clothes may be at the camp."

"Do you think he is old enough to be so employed?" she asked.

"He is quite large enough," the man answered. "He may be young, but I judge him to be taller by a head than I."

"Look at his face, Lemuel. He has not yet begun a

beard. I doubt he has seen his fourteenth summer."

As Walker lay there he thought about the names he was hearing. Lemuel, Sally, Elisha, Eunice, Daniel, Peter. All were names he had heard during the cemetery ghost walks. Lemuel and Sally Taylor were the first settlers of Stony Creek. They were Walker's great-great-great–how many 'greats' Walker wasn't sure— grandparents. Elisha Taylor was the son that had staked out the land in 1822. Eunice and Daniel were the Taylor's youngest children, the only ones not married when the family arrived in 1823. Peter Groesbeck was the blacksmith.

Walker remained on his back and closed his eyes. The thought that he may have been thrown back in time to the 1820s made his head spin. There must be other, more reasonable possibilities. He tried to sort them out.

It's all too real to be a dream, he thought. Maybe it's a hoax. Yeah, that's it. But why would anyone go to all this trouble to make me think I've gone 180 years back in time? Whatever their reason, these people are up to something. Maybe they're all from an insane asylum. Or maybe I just got washed downstream right into the middle of it. I'd better be careful. If they can put on an act like this, who knows what else they could do?

Walker was getting scared. All he wanted was to get himself out of there. Tossing the blanket aside, he got to his hands and knees. But before he could get up, he began another coughing spell.

"Take my hand," the man said, helping Walker to his feet. "Perhaps you will feel better after a cup of Mrs. Taylor's soup."

"Could you get me to the hospital?" Walker said, rising slowly.

"Hospital?" the man said. "There is but one doctor within two days of here."

I must be miles downstream, Walker thought. He studied the bank that followed the curve of the creek. It sure looks like my fishing hole. He glanced across the stream and up the hill to where Renee's house should be. There was nothing but trees and brush. His eyes settled on the area where he thought he left his bicycle by the bridge. Yes, I'm sure that's it. But there was no bike. There was no bridge! The road leading up the hill was only a narrow path.

"Are you able to walk to the house?" the woman said, pointing to the small cabin in the distance.

"I guess," Walker said, taking his first wobbly step.

"It appears that you will recover," the bearded man said. "My name is Lemuel Taylor and this is my wife Sarah. What is your name, son?"

At the straight-forward introduction to two people who had been dead for nearly two hundred years, Walker broke into a cold sweat. Blood drained from his head and dropped like mercury to his feet. He stared first at the bearded man and then at the gentle-faced woman. Walker's eyes rolled and his knees felt like silly putty. He gazed at the crude log cabin that stood where the large, two-story museum should have been. The ground began to spin. The trees and sky whirled into a sea of green and blue. With his next step, Walker lurched forward and fell flat on his face.

Chapter 4

🖋 *The Truth* 🖋

"I believe the boy has fainted, Sally," the man said. "Perhaps you should stay with him while I fetch the salts."

The man hurried to the log cabin and returned in minutes with a small, glass container. He loosened the cork and waved it under Walker's nose.

Walker's head snapped back. He opened his eyes. "Where am I? What's that awful smell?" Walker said, getting to his knees.

"Spirits of nitre," the man said.

"It smells like the boys' john," Walker mumbled. He glanced at the two people and remembered his eerie predicament. If they were trying to pull a trick on him, they were hiding it well. They seemed to be truly worried about him. Walker suddenly wished that the nasty odor in the tiny vial was the worst of his problems.

"You must remove your wet garments and get into something warm before you catch your death," the woman said. "I shall ask Nathaniel if he has an extra pair of trousers that you may wear. He is the only man tall enough here at Stony Creek whose clothes would fit you."

"You are looking better, though," the man said. "Maybe now you can tell us where you live."

"Rochester," Walker whispered hoarsely. "Fourth and Walnut. Do you know where that is?"

"Rochester? Yes, indeed, I do," the man said. "It is a mile south and a half mile west of here."

"Well, if you could point me in that direction," Walker said, "I think I can find my way home."

"That would be ill-advised, son," the man said, shaking his head. "Many bears and wolves lurk in the forest along the trail. Their hunger is great this time of the year. You would be easy prey. Perhaps you should wait and accompany us on our weekly journey there tomorrow."

Weekly journey? Walker thought. A mile and a half into Rochester? Man, this guy is either totally whacked out, or I really am in the 1820s. But that can't be. You don't just get dunked under water for ten seconds and come up 180 years earlier. I'll bet he's one of those religious kooks. This must be his cult hideout. I'd better not rile him. Someone called him Reverend Taylor, so if he is the leader and I push the wrong button, he might do something really weird. I'd better just play along with whatever he says. Besides, until I find my bike I've got no fast way out of here. If I can talk to some of those other people, maybe that boy and little girl, I could trick them into telling me the truth. At least it would buy me some time to sort things out.

"I guess you're right" Walker said. "I am cold, and I really don't feel so good. Maybe I'll take you up on that soup you were talking about."

"That would be nice," the woman said with a smile. "A cup of my special soup will make you fit as a fiddle in no time."

Special soup, eh? Walker thought. She's probably going to fill it with sleeping powder or poison. What have I gotten myself into?

"Perhaps you will feel better later and help us with some of our tasks," the man said. "We have much to do before the snow flies. If our work is not completed by winter, some of our members will surely perish from lack of food or proper shelter."

"Right," Walker said, rolling his eyes. He immediately realized how sarcastic he had sounded, but the thought of somebody in the Rochester area dying from lack of food or housing was laughable.

Walker glanced around for a road out of the area. There were no streets, sidewalks, bikepaths—nothing. He became flustered for a moment and dropped his guard. "Maybe I could call my parents from your phone," Walker said.

"Phone?" the man asked.

That was dumb, Walker thought. The old guy is too much into this history reenactment thing to fall for that. He seems to be getting annoyed. I'd better not mess with him any more.

"Yeah, you know, a megaphone," Walker said, trying to cover his mistake. "Like cheerleaders have." They must at least have cheerleaders. It's a large cone-shaped thing that you yell into. People can hear you from a long ways away."

"No, I assure you that we would have no use for a 'megaphone,' as you call it," the man said. "Come along now."

Man, oh man, this isn't going very well, Walker thought. I don't want to rile the old bugger. If I really did get tossed back into the nineteenth century, he could run me out of here. I wouldn't want any part of those bears and wolves he was talking about. I've never much cared for things that lurk in the woods.

Walker staggered up the hill between the man and woman. The roughly hewn log cabin was made like a duplex—two houses put together with a breezeway separating them but with one roof covering both.

"This is where our son Elisha, and his family live," the lady said, pointing to the door on the left. "Our two youngest children, Daniel and Eunice, live here with us. As small as it is, it is still much nicer than the shanty we made last spring to get us through until our crops were planted."

From the outside there wasn't a trace of any modern building materials: no thermopane windows, no screens, no aluminum siding, no TV dishes. Walker followed the man and woman through the door. Inside was worse. The whole place was only about twenty feet square, smaller than Walker's living room. The floor wasn't just dirty, it was all dirt–flat, hard-packed dirt. Someone had drawn a design in it to make it look like a braided rug. How pathetic, Walker thought. They're too poor to buy a carpet.

Walker glanced around for a TV, a radio, a microwave—even a lamp. But there were none. He looked for electrical outlets, plumbing, ventilation ducts, but there were none of those, either. This house isn't even code! The building inspector would have a field day if he ever caught up with these yahoos.

A fireplace was built along the far wall. There were three cots, you could not really call them beds, and a table with six chairs near a wooden sink. Four oil lamps hung from the ceiling. Walker noticed a set of ladder rungs leading up to a loft where he could see two more cots. Instead of glass windows, boards were nailed together, hinged at the top, and propped open with sticks. Flies buzzed all over the place. Even though it was tolerably warm outside, inside it was cool and damp, reminding Walker of his basement where he and his friends played video games on hot summer days.

"Here, this will help," the lady said, handing Walker a crude earthenware bowl and wooden spoon. She smiled politely, but Walker thought that her body language was trying to warn him about "Reverend Taylor" and his fiendish followers.

Walker took the bowl. The condemned man's last meal, he thought, the beginning of the end. I'll just pretend to taste it. He took a sniff. It smelled great. He suddenly realized that he hadn't eaten anything since the two slices of pepperoni pizza he had for lunch at the school cafeteria, and he had just puked that all over the place down by the creek. Now he was starved. He took another whiff. He couldn't resist tasting it. It was terrific. It was no Big Mac and fries, but darned good. The bowl was filled to the top with large chunks of meat and potatoes.

Walker sat down at the table and put the wooden spoon to work. He ladled the stew into his mouth like there was no tomorrow. As he did, he heard a latch creak behind him. He turned and saw two small heads poking through the doorway.

"We are done weeding, Mother," the boy said. "Can we look at the strange visitor?"

"Come in, children," the woman said with a laugh. "Sit at the table with our guest. I will ask Nathaniel about some clothes."

"I must return to the mill," the bearded man said. "The others are gathering to set the stone into place. You children may chat with Mister . . . . You know, son, you have not told us your name."

"Morrison," Walker said, spooning in the last of the poisonous soup. "Walker Morrison." What could that hurt? Walker thought. I'm dead already.

"Good," the man said. "You children may show Mr. Morrison around the village. You look to be feeling better, Walker."

At that, the elderly couple left the cabin. The man went down the hill toward the stream, and the woman hurried in the opposite direction toward a log house in the distance. Walker stood in the middle of the room. The boy and girl stared at him, their mouths hanging open as if he were a Barnum and Bailey Circus freak.

Well, here's my chance, Walker thought. If I can trip these kids up with just one mistake, it will prove everything is a hoax. Then I'll run for all I'm worth. It won't matter which way—just out of here.

"Where do you guys go to school, I mean, when you're not out here doing these history things with your parents?" Walker asked, watching each of them for a reaction.

"We do not have a school yet," Daniel said. "Not a real one. We take turns each day going to neighbors' houses. We older kids have lessons in the winter. The younger ones go in the summer. My father says that soon we will have a teacher and a real schoolhouse, maybe even this fall. Until then we study the assignments that he makes up for us. We just got here last spring, you know. We came from Aurelius in New York State."

"Really," Walker said. "How'd you get here—plane,

boat, car?"

Daniel stared at Walker with a puzzled look. "I do not know what a 'plain boat' is," Daniel said. "We took a barge on the Erie Canal and crossed Lake Erie on the *Superior*, a brand new steamboat. Then we took a schooner up into Lake Saint Clair where a terrible storm almost blew us onto the Flats, that's what Captain Miller called it, until my father—he is a preacher, you know—he had us kneel down to pray. All the while Captain Miller was cursing at his crew to let out more sail. Somehow we made it to Mount Clemens. Then we went up the Clinton River as far as it could take us. After that we came here by ox cart. One of my older brothers, Elisha, had staked the claim on this land the summer before last."

Walker stared in disbelief. Unless this kid has been totally brainwashed by that old bearded guy, there is no way he could know all this stuff. He's telling it just like my dad, only with a lot more detail. I've never heard anyone say that the name of the steamboat was the *Superior*, or that Mr. Miller was the captain of the schooner. If this kid's not telling the truth, he's doing an awesome job of faking it.

"Now it is your turn," the little girl said looking at Walker. "How did you get here?"

"Good question. Uh, what was your name again?" Walker said. He knew they had called her Eunice, but he wanted the kids to be doing the talking, not him.

32

Besides, his dad had told him he was descended directly from Eunice Taylor. Even if he found out she was a fake, it would be fun listening to her tell her story.

She stood straight and tall. "My name is Eunice Taylor," she said excitedly. "I am eight years old, but I am as strong as any ten-year-old boy. Just ask Daniel. He will tell you."

"Oh, I believe you," Walker said. He turned to the boy. "And how old are you, Daniel?"

"I am twelve," Daniel said, staring uneasily at Walker. "But wo want to know about you. How did you get here?"

The two boys' eyes locked. Neither blinked but searched the other for several seconds. Finally, Daniel turned to the little girl.

"Eunice," he said, "I believe Walker is getting cold from his wet clothes. Would you mind going over to Nate's cabin and finding Mom?"

"Do I have to?" Eunice pouted. She gave her brother a defiant stare. He nodded.

Eunice stomped her feet, pulled the door open, and made a beeline for a distant cabin.

Chapter 5

∗ *Tales* ∗

"I'm not feeling so good," Walker said to Daniel. Too many points were piling up to prove that he had somehow landed in the 1820s. "Let's go outside. I need some air."

The two left the cabin and went down the hill. At the river bank they sat facing each other on two tree stumps.

"Listen, Daniel," Walker said anxiously. "This is really important. Can you keep a secret?"

"I believe I can," Daniel said.

"Good, because if what you're telling me is true, then I'm going to have a heck of a time making people believe, not where I'm from, but when I'm from."

"When you are from?" Daniel said, raising an eyebrow.

"Yeah, when," Walker said. "Let's start with this. What day is today?"

"Friday," Daniel said.

"No, I mean, what's the date?"

"Oh, uh, May 20th, I think," Daniel said.

"And the year?"

"Eighteen-twenty-four," Daniel said. "Why? What year did you think it was?"

Daniel's candid answer was the final straw. "Not that one," Walker said. He took in a deep breath and let it out slowly. He looked across the landscape and recognized that this was, in fact, his favorite fishing place. It looked just like it would before 180 years of civilization had brought physical changes to the area. Walker was now convinced that he had indeed gone back almost two centuries in time.

"Daniel," Walker whispered, "please promise that you won't tell a soul what I'm about to tell you?"

"You are not a British spy or a murderer or anything, are you?" Daniel Taylor asked.

British spy? Man, how things have changed. "No," Walker said, "it's nothing like that."

"Then I promise," Daniel said. "What is the secret?"

Well, here goes, Walker thought. I've got to have someone I can talk to, someone I can trust. Who better than my own great-great-great-grand uncle? "When I came over that hill this afternoon," Walker said, pointing toward Rochester, "it was Friday, May 20, 2002. That, Daniel, is 178 years into your future." Walker leaned back, letting that thought sink in with his young ancestor.

Daniel's eyes opened wide in amazement.

"I came here to fish," Walker said, "like I have hundreds of times since I was a little kid. I come here because it's a darned good trout stream. Also, because my dad says that our family is directly related to the people who settled it—the Lemuel Taylor family—your family. You, Daniel, are my great- great-great-grand uncle. What's more, and I have seen this on my family tree, I'm the great-great-great grandson of Eunice Taylor, your little sister."

Daniel's mouth dropped open. "My little sister?" he finally said. "How could you be Eunice's great-great-great grandson? That is impossible. She is just a little girl."

"Yeah, I know. It's all impossible," Walker said. "One minute I'm fly-fishing in my favorite trout stream in 2002, and the next I'm lying on the ground, choking my head off like I swallowed a gallon of jet fuel and blowing pepperoni pizza all over the neighborhood. And, incidentally, it just happens to be 1824."

Daniel stared at Walker.

"You've got to believe me," Walker pleaded. Tears were welling up in his eyes.

Daniel nodded. "I do," he said. "What you are telling me is too unreal not to believe. But my parents? I do not believe you can convince them. And I do not think you should try, at least for awhile. You use many strange words, Walker. If we are to keep your secret, you will need to speak as we do. People do not expect me to say much because I am only twelve years old. But you are as big as any grown man. How old are you?"

"Thirteen," Walker said.

"You are only thirteen?" Daniel said in surprise.

Walker nodded.

"Well," Daniel said, "your size alone makes you a man in their eyes. They will ask you what you think about many things."

"Yeah, you're right," Walker said. "I keep hoping that this is all a dream, and I'll wake up any minute. Maybe, if I can just get back to Rochester, I'll find my way to my own time."

"Maybe," Daniel said, "but until then, folks will want to know all about you. It is just the neighborly thing to do. If you tell them that you have lost your parents, they will do anything to help you find them. But if you tell them that your parents have not been born yet, they won't have much patience. We came with only enough supplies to get us through one winter, so we have to make every day count."

"You mean, if they learn my secret they will turn me out?" Walker said, sitting up.

"I am afraid so," Daniel said. "But you must be here for a reason."

"What do you mean?" Walker asked.

"My father says that everything happens for a reason. It says so in the Bible. Ecclesiastes, I think."

"All right, you tell me," Walker said. "Why would I have been sent 178 years back in time?"

"I do not know," Daniel said with a shrug, "but as

long as we can keep your secret, you need not worry about being turned out from Stony Creek. We have lots of work to do—crops to plant and harvest, tools to make, livestock to tend, mills to build. And there are all the regular chores every day."

"I've never done any of those things," Walker said.

"Really?" Daniel said, a smile crossing his lips. "Do not tell me you tat and stitch, knit and sew, all those girl things."

"No, of course not," Walker said, stiffening his back. "Mostly I go to school and play sports. I'm on the football and swimming teams. On weekends I chill out with my friends. We watch TV, listen to CDs, play video games, go to the mall. Stuff like that."

Daniel looked confused. "After the 'school' part, I did not understand a word you said."

"Look, all I can tell you is that I don't know how I can help around here. Maybe if we can make them believe I'm from 2002, they won't expect much. All I'd have to do is talk about what it's like in the future."

"I do not think that would work," Daniel said. "Put yourself in their place. If I came over the hill into Rochester 178 years from now and told everyone that I had just dropped in from 1824, how long do you think it would take before they locked me up? Folks would be out right now gathering armfuls of kindling to burn me at the stake for witchcraft. They would fight for the chance to light the fire. Am I right?"

"We don't burn people in my time," Walker said. "Besides, I didn't just come over the hill. You were there. Your dad saved me, remember?"

"I know, but people who did not see it happen will think that was a trick, too. They will think you are trying to get something out of them. Or worse, they will think you are insane. Either way, no one will believe you unless you have proof."

Walker reached into his pockets. A coin would do. A recent mintmark would be on it. Walker tried all his pockets but found not oven a penny. He pulled off his fishing jacket and looked for a patent label, something with a date. No luck.

"I don't have anything except what I know," Walker said.

"All right," Daniel said. "Until we figure out how to get you back where you belong, you have a home here. As long as we can keep your secret, my parents would never turn you away."

"Okay," Walker said, his spirits brightening. "But I sure wish this hadn't happened."

"For your sake, I do too," Daniel said. "But for now, at least, I have a new friend—one like no one has ever had—one from another time and with more great stories than anyone else in all the world."

"You'll do it?" Walker said. "You'll keep my secret?"

"If you can, I can," Daniel said, and the two shook hands.

Chapter 6

✺ *The Test* ✺

"Here comes my mother," Daniel said. "It looks as if she has found some real clothes for you, Walker. Dry ones, too."

"I hope these will fit," Mrs. Taylor said as she and Eunice approached the two boys. She handed Walker a whole outfit of socks, pants, shirt, and shoes. "Come inside. You may change in the loft. Bring your wet clothes down when you are done. I will try to mend them."

"Thank you, Mrs. Taylor," Walker said. He called her by her name for the first time and thought of her as who she really was, his great-great-great-great grand-mother.

"There's one thing you boys can do," she said. She turned to Daniel. "Your father could use your help at the mill. He needs every hand he can get to set the milling stone into place."

Walker climbed the wall ladder with his new clothes slung over his shoulder. Stepping onto the loft floor to check out his surroundings, he immediately banged his head on a ceiling beam. He looked for another place to stand, but there was nowhere in the loft that he would be able to stand straight.

He spread the brown-and-beige plaid shirt, white woolen pants, and long, white socks on the narrow bed. He stripped off his torn clothes and blown-out tennis shoes. First, he put on the loose-fitting linen underpants, tying them with a drawstring. Next, he pulled the coarse scratchy breeches over his legs. He glanced down and noticed the pant legs reached only to his knees. This Nathaniel guy must be a midget, Walker thought. Then he remembered how Mr. Taylor and the other men dressed. They all wore short baggy pants with long white socks.

Walker stood to zip his trousers. He looked down at the crotch. There was no zipper! There were buttons and holes all over the place, from his waist to his knees. But there was nothing but air at the fly. He figured out the knee buttons, used to keep his socks up—but none of the others matched the holes. Finally, he got enough of them to line up so that the pants didn't fall down.

"Is something wrong?" Daniel called from below.

"No. Everything's cool," Walker said as he fastened the last button. He wasn't sure if Mrs. Taylor was still in the cabin or if she had gone outside. He wanted to ask Daniel for help getting the pants on, but he was afraid that if Mrs. Taylor heard, she would think it odd that he couldn't dress himself.

Next, he looked at the shirt. It was much simpler

than the trousers. It had only one button at the top. He pulled the shirt over his head and tucked in the long tails. It was full and loose, not at all like the tailored, button-down shirts he wore when he dressed for church, and even less like the tee-shirt he had shredded in the tree while fishing. He left the button undone just as Daniel did with his shirt.

Walker looked at the plain, black leather boots. He set them next to his old size 13 Reebok cross-trainers. No way were they going to fit. Who'd they think he was, Cinderella? If Nathaniel was the tallest person in the village, he probably had the biggest feet, too. Walker realized that, for now at least, he would have to go barefoot like Daniel and Eunice.

Walker pulled off the long socks, grabbed his old, wet clothes, and made his way down the ladder. Mrs. Taylor was gone, so he turned to Daniel. "Well, how do I look?" he asked.

A smirk crept over Daniel's face. "Fine, Walker. You look just fine. That is, if you do not mind going outside and meeting everyone with your breeches on backwards."

"What?" Walker said, glancing down. He looked at how Daniel had buttoned his trousers.

In seconds the pants were reversed, and Walker and Daniel were out the door. They ran the short distance from the cabin to the stream and over to a flat platform made of thick wooden planks. Lemuel Taylor and five other men stood knee-deep in the stream. On the bank of the river lay a flat, round stone four feet across and a foot thick with a six-inch square hole in the middle.

"We are almost ready," Lemuel Taylor said as Walker and Daniel approached. "Men, this is Walker Morrison. Some of you were with us this afternoon. Were it not for the grace of God, he would have drowned." He turned to Walker. "How are you feeling, son?"

"Better, sir," Walker said. "Thank you." Walker looked at the bearded man much differently than he had only an hour before. This is really Reverend Lemuel Taylor, Walker thought. This is the founder of Stony Creek, my great-great-great-great grandfather. Without him this whole area would not be the same.

"I will introduce you to the other men later," Mr. Taylor said. "Now we must hoist this grinding stone into place. It weighs over sixteen hundred pounds, so it will be no easy task moving it into position."

Walker eyed the granite boulder and then the eight men, Daniel and himself included, who would do the lifting. He did some quick math. Sixteen hundred pounds divided by eight. That's two hundred pounds each. Walker had never lifted more than a hundred and fifty pounds, and that was in the Hart training room where the weights had handles. This stone did not. There was no way they'd be able to hoist this dead weight onto the platform. He glanced at the men nearby. None of them looked very strong. They were, in fact, on the scrawny side. No Incredible Hulks here. And Mr. Taylor had to be over sixty years old. Still, none of them seemed worried about it.

Mr. Taylor set the places for each of the men around the stone. Daniel and Walker stood opposite each other. At Mr. Taylor's signal, all eight bent down, grabbed hold, and lifted. Walker strained, his eyes closed, and realized the stone was off the ground. When it got to his waist, he opened his eyes and looked across at Daniel who was grinning like an Olympic weight-lifting champion.

"Let us begin," Lemuel said. The eight men walked up a ramp to the platform that would be the floor of the mill. They carried their stone directly above an identical slab of granite that had a six-inch square iron peg sticking through its middle.

"Slowly now," Lemuel said. "This has to fit perfectly."

Beads of sweat ran into Walker's eyes as the men lowered the stone onto the peg. A final grunt signalled that it was in place. They had done it! A wave of euphoria swept over him. He felt more like part of a winning team than after any of his swimming meets or football victories.

Walker was sure this amazing feat would be celebrated with some macho, nineteenth century form of high-fiving among the men. He half expected someone to be sneaking up from behind Mr. Taylor with a drum of Gatorade to dump over his head. Instead, when he turned back, the men were walking away, heading toward their own tasks.

Lemuel Taylor stood with Walker and Daniel. "You two made the difference," he said. "Thank you, Walker. You are a strong young man. I suppose you will be wanting to get on your way soon, but I still would like to know how you came here. Are you working on a government survey crew?"

"No, sir," Walker said. "I'm not working for anyone."

"How about family?" Mr. Taylor continued. "You said you are from Rochester. Do you live near here?"

Walker glanced at Daniel and then back to Mr. Taylor. "Not as near as I'd like," Walker said. "Fact is, I'm kind of lost. Maybe I could stay here for a while. I would work for room and board."

"We could use another man," Mr. Taylor said, tugging his beard. "There is much to be done. I will need help finishing this mill. It must be completed before we harvest our corn." Mr. Taylor turned to Daniel. "Do you think there is enough room in the loft?"

"Sure," Daniel said. "Harry's spare bed is already up there."

"Then it is settled," Lemuel Taylor said. "Let us get a few of these corner beams into place, and we will go up to the house for supper."

Walker followed Mr. Taylor and Daniel to a pile of roughly- hewn, eight-by-eight inch timbers. For the first time ever, Walker had a real feeling of achievement and, strangely enough, a sense of belonging. Not that he hadn't felt wanted by his parents, but he'd never felt needed by them. The closest thing was when he helped at the store on Saturdays, or when he caught a few good-sized trout and brought them home to eat. This, however, was a very different kind of need, another feeling altogether.

Chapter 7

❦ *Rodeo Rider* ❧

Walker, Daniel, and Mr. Taylor set the four corner beams into place for the outline of the mill. Mr. Taylor stood back and examined their handiwork. "This has been a fine day," he said. "Perhaps you boys would like to go out to the barn and help Eunice bring in the eggs. She should be about done gathering them. Then, being Friday, we shall have supper, rest, and prepare our list for the trip into Rochester tomorrow."

Rochester. Walker's heart skipped a beat when he heard the name. What will it be like? Maybe everything there will be normal and this whole weird deal at Stony Creek will be over, he thought as he and Daniel walked toward the barn. He pictured the town as he had left it that afternoon—Main Street, his dad's store, his house. Then he thought about his encounter with Renee St. Jean. That reminded him of Kenny Fisher. The two of them were probably playing volleyball at the park right now where he would be if he hadn't decided to go fishing. Kenny was sure to ask Renee to the last dance of the spring term.

The two boys crossed the yard with Mr. Taylor. The

bearded man went inside the cabin. Walker and Daniel continued toward the small barn. Daniel went ahead and pulled its door open. A blast of hot smelly air poured out and smacked Walker in the face, practically knocking him over. His eyes began to water from the awful fumes.

The last time he'd been in a barn was about six years ago when his first grade class took a field trip to a farm near Oxford. Like all city kids Walker and his classmates had seen cows and horses and chickens. They knew what sounds they made. They could tell what they tasted like when they were cooked and served on a plate in a dining room. But they had never actually smelled the animals in their own environment. Walker's class was totally unprepared for the overwhelming stench.

Some of the kids pinched their noses. Some began to cry. Walker just turned tail, squinted his eyes, and ran as fast as he could back to the school bus.

The odor was too much for him then, and it was almost too much for him now. He stood outside the barn as Daniel went in.

"Come on," Daniel said, turning and seeing Walker's glazed expression. "What is wrong? You look sick."

"Nothing, I'm okay," Walker said stepping forward. "Where are the eggs?"

"Right here," Daniel said, pointing to a wire basket. "But I do not see Eunice." He looked all around.

"Eunice!" he called. "Where are you?"

"I am here," a voice chirped from above.

Walker looked straight up and saw Eunice balancing on a beam directly over his head.

"What are you doing?" Daniel asked. He sounded annoyed.

"Waiting for you," she said with a teasing laugh. "I dare you to go bareback on Daisy."

"I am not riding any cows," Daniel said. "It is too dangerous, and besides, dinner is almost ready."

"Scaredy cat," Eunice taunted.

"Am not," Daniel said, his voice rising at the insult. "It just so happens that I am smart enough to know a stupid stunt when I see one. Come down from there before you break your neck."

"I double dare you," Eunice persisted. "Here comes Daisy now."

Walker turned and watched a small brown cow enter from the pasture through a wide door at the other end of the barn. Eunice ran along the wide beam eight feet above the ground and stopped directly over the unsuspecting Guernsey heifer.

"Look out below!" Eunice yelled as she dropped from the timber. She fell squarely on the cow's back with her legs straddling its flanks.

Daisy leapt in surprise with all four hooves leaving the ground. She spun halfway around, facing the door to the pasture. Eunice let out a squeal and held on with both hands as the two streaked out of the barn and across the clover field. The cow raced for a big chestnut tree about thirty yards away. One low branch stuck straight out, just high enough to scrape Eunice from Daisy's back.

"Jump!" Daniel yelled.

At the last moment Eunice leaped from Daisy's back and rolled in the soft meadow. She bounced up facing the boys and waved her hands in the air. "Yah-hoo!" she yelled, and started to run toward Walker and Daniel who stood in stunned silence. "Now it's your turn," she added from a distance.

"She is always doing foolish tricks like that," Daniel said to Walker as Eunice made her way toward them. "She will do anything to prove that she is as tough as any boy. One day it will get her into trouble."

"Did you hear me?" Eunice yelled, running up to her brother. "It is your turn. You must do it next."

"No, I do not," Daniel replied calmly. "First of all, I did not take your dare. Besides, I am not stupid enough to try a fool trick like that."

"Scaredy cat," Eunice sneered.

"Am not," Daniel said, picking up the basket of eggs.

Walker, who still hadn't recovered from either the smell of the barn or Eunice's near miss with the tree, was only too glad to follow the Taylor kids back to the cabin. He was getting hungry and looked forward to finding out what Mrs. Taylor had cooked for supper.

Chapter 8

❧ *First Evening* ❧

Mrs. Taylor was setting the table as Eunice, Walker, and Daniel came across the yard from the barn. The two Taylor kids each had a bounce in their steps as if they were just getting warmed up for something else. Walker, on the other hand, barely dragged himself through the door before collapsing into one of the straight-backed, wooden chairs next to the hearth.

"Walker, you look as if you have had a long day," Mrs. Taylor said as she carried the venison stew and boiled turnips to the table.

"I'm okay," Walker said, wondering what she would think if he told her how long his day had really been.

"Supper is ready," said Mrs. Taylor.

"Let us gather round the table," Mr. Taylor said more for Walker's sake than for the others who were already standing behind their chairs.

Walker noticed that everyone was waiting for him. At the sight of the food he found new life. He sprang from the chair by the fireplace and went to the unoccupied place between Daniel and Eunice. He began to sit down but Daniel grabbed his arm and pulled him to an abrupt halt.

"Let us bow our heads," Mr. Taylor said with a look of surprise at the newcomer. Walker lowered his head and listened as Reverend Taylor blessed the food, the day, the family, the community, and the chance to serve the Lord in every way Walker believed was possible. Finally, when Walker didn't think he could resist the smell of the stew any longer, Mr. Taylor said his amen.

The rest of the Taylors repeated their amen in unison. Walker was off by about a beat and a half, but what followed was the best tasting meal he ever had. It didn't look like much, but the gravy was thick and the meat nearly melted in his mouth. Even the green stuff, whatever it was, tasted good. Between bites every Taylor told what he or she had done that day and what was going on with the rest of the Stony Creek people.

Walker began to think about his own family and how rarely they all sat at the kitchen table—or did anything together for that matter. Someone was always going off to a ball practice, or a meeting, or over to a friend's house. Even when they did eat dinner together, the phone was always ringing and the television blaring the world's most shocking news. They never just talked, or asked questions, or told about something that had happened during their day. Walker guessed that when stacked up against all the amazing events on television, everything he wanted to say was unimportant, at least to his brothers who had formed some sort of Vulcan mind-meld with the TV while they inhaled their food. After Walker used his last scrap of bread to sop up his gravy, he looked around for a place to stretch out. He had never been so beat in all his life. The inside of the cabin was getting dark, so Mrs. Taylor lit a candle. She brought it to the table and set it next to a thin leather-bound book and slate.

"Time for your ciphering lesson, Daniel," she said.

It's Friday night, Walker thought. Who does homework on Friday nights? It wasn't his problem though, and Daniel didn't seem to mind.

"Would you like to sit down, Walker?" Mrs. Taylor said. "If you already know how to do this, perhaps you could help teach it to Daniel."

"Ciphering? Sure, yeah, be glad to," Walker said, not having the slightest idea what 'ciphering' was. He was certain that it had to be about five generations easier than the seventh grade math and science he had been taking this past school year. He'd often thought how easy school must have been in the olden days. American history, for example. Right now in 1824 kids had, what, fifty years of stuff to learn? And American Lit— almost no one had written anything yet, so how hard could that be?

As Daniel opened the book, Walker glanced over his shoulder. It was a math lesson. Walker watched as Daniel began to "cipher." It was like nothing Walker had ever seen before, a nineteenth century version of

New Math. Nothing made sense to him, but Daniel zipped through the questions in no time at all. Even if Walker had his calculator he couldn't have beaten Daniel to the answers.

"You're pretty good at this," Walker whispered.

"Well, if I am to help my father at the mill, I must learn how to charge the customer for what he gets. If I make a mistake in our favor, the customer will catch it and think I am trying to cheat him. If I make a mistake in his favor, we will lose money. Either way it is not good business."

Walker nodded. He'd heard his dad say the same thing at the drug store—only instead of with a prescription customer it was with some huge insurance company thousands of miles away.

"Tomorrow," Mr. Taylor said, looking up from his Bible as he sat by the fireplace, "a few of the men will be going into Rochester. Would you like to join us, Walker?"

As bushed as Walker was he opened his eyes wide and said, "Sure." This might be my chance, he thought. Maybe I'll see someone there that I recognize–my dad at the pharmacy, Mr. Kania at the tire place, or Dr. Wiseman at the foot clinic, and I'll suddenly be back in 2002. This is all so weird that I don't know what will happen.

"May I go, too?" Daniel asked.

"Yes, if you would like," Mr. Taylor said. "We will be

leaving at sunrise."

"Then we had best be hitting the hay, Walker," Daniel said. "Follow me to the loft."

"What if we get into town and everything is how it was when I left there?" Walker whispered to Daniel as each pulled his wool blanket away from his corn husk mattress. "What if you are the ones that are out of place and I'm the one at home?"

"I do not know, Walker," Daniel said as he eased himself into his bed. "I still am having trouble believing all the things you have told me. If we get near Rochester and I see anything that is at all strange, I might just hop off the wagon and run back here, wolves and bears or not."

"Yeah, it sure will be different for one of us," Walker said with a yawn. "Let's get to sleep."

Chapter 9

Night Thoughts

The day's heat had collected in the stuffy cabin loft. Walker knew he was in for a long hot night. Daniel had carried a candle up the ladder and set it on a table between their cots. As Walker sat on the edge of his bed he heard the hum of mosquitoes zeroing in on his ankles and neck. Walker's first notion was to burrow under the covers. On the other hand, the heat and humidity of the room made him wish he were somewhere in the Arctic. He stripped to his shorts and stared at the lumpy mattress filled with corn husks. He would be a lot happier at home in his Serta Perfect Sleeper with the windows closed and the air conditioner going full blast.

Still, Walker was too tired to give it much thought. He stretched out and sank slowly into the lumpy, crinkling mattress. "Good night, Walker," Daniel said as he blew the candle out.

"Night, Daniel."

The flame flickered and everything went black. Walker felt as if he'd been whisked into the deepest cavern in the planet. He opened his eyes and closed them. There was no difference.

In Walker's house something was always lit—an electric alarm clock, a bathroom night light, the shaft of the street lamp filtering in through the window shades, or just a TV channel number on the cable box.There was some light somewhere. For the first time in his life he could look in every direction and not see anything. He held his hand in front of his eyes. He waved it right up to his nose. He even touched it. There was nothing but black.

He began to think about his home, his friends, and his family. His dad would need him to work at the store the next morning. Saturday was the one day Walker knew he was really needed. Most of the regular employees had the weekends off. On Saturdays it could get really hectic. If Walker stayed here in 1824, his dad would be short-handed.

Man, oh man, Walker thought, how did I get myself into such a fix? He turned onto his stomach. He tossed and rolled some more. Then he began to think about his mom. She probably was frantic by now. She was sure to have a search party out after him, but Walker knew no matter how many people were out there combing the area, they wouldn't be able to look 178 years into the past.

Then there was Renee. Talk about rotten luck. Just when he finally meets the foxiest babe in the known universe, he pulls a vanishing act. There Kenny would be, Mr. Smooth, helping her recover from the emotional shock of Walker's tragic disappearance. For sure Kenny would be taking her to the last school dance.

That reminded Walker about his classes. He had to get back for the last couple weeks or he wouldn't get into the eighth grade. His stomach actually turned a complete flip-flop when he thought about having to repeat seventh grade. It turned practically inside out when he realized that he might never get back. He might be stuck here for the rest of his life.

Before he drifted to sleep he pictured his tombstone next to Lemuel Taylor's in the Stony Creek cemetery. It read:

Walker Alexander Morrison
Born 1989–Died 1884
Age 73
A Man Born After His Time.

Walker was in a deep sleep when he felt someone nudge his shoulder. He blinked and saw a dim figure leaning over him.

"Rise and shine. We must hurry if we are to go to Rochester."

Walker was still more than half asleep. "Mom?" he croaked.

He rolled on the crunchy mattress. This isn't my bed. He looked more closely at the person standing over him. That's not Mom. It all came back in a flash. He wasn't in his own house, or town, or even his own century!

Walker struggled out of the cot. He could hear bacon and eggs crackling in a frying pan downstairs. He had never awakened to a more wonderful smell. His mom would never make bacon and eggs for breakfast. She had read in some health magazine that neither eggs nor bacon were good for you, so it was rare that Walker would get either one for breakfast. It was unheard of to get both at once.

The strong aroma of fresh-brewed coffee also wafted up from below. That would never happen in his house, either. His mother had also read a government study that said coffee was bad for people. He had tasted it once and didn't doubt it for a second, but it always smelled like "morning" when he was a kid. He remembered his dad sitting over his cup on Saturday mornings as he read the *Oakland Press* before going to the store.

The combined smells of bacon, eggs, and coffee made Walker bounce out of his lumpy bed. Enough predawn light filtered into the cabin to help him see his way around the loft. He was now fully awake. He knew where he was and where he was going, to Rochester, hopefully to find his home and family.

Walker reached for his pants. He made sure he had them on frontwards before struggling with the buttons. He pulled his shirt over his head and searched for his socks and shoes before remembering that he didn't have any. His feet were sore from going barefoot the day before, but he had enjoyed the feeling of walking in the warm mud and soft clover without them. And if he came in from outside with mud on his feet, so what? Walker reasoned that a dirt floor can't get much dirtier than it already is. These pioneers were really on to something with this. He moved to the ladder, bumped his head once again on the ceiling, and followed Daniel downstairs.

Mr. and Mrs. Taylor were sitting at the table. Mr. Taylor looked up as Walker turned and faced them. "Good morning, Walker," Mr. Taylor said. The tone of his voice was somber and caused Walker to pause.

"Good morning, Mr. Taylor," Walker said. He searched Lemuel Taylor's eyes for a clue to the serious nature of his greeting.

"Walker?" Mr. Taylor said.

"Yes, sir?"

"Please try to understand," the Reverend said, "I am not sure what it is you are holding back from us, but I want you to know that when you are ready to tell me I will be here to listen."

Walker leaned against the ladder. He glanced at Daniel. Had Daniel told on him? But Daniel looked surprised and Walker could tell that he had not.

"Yes, sir," Walker said.

"We will be meeting the other men when the sun comes up," Lemuel Taylor said. "Remember we are all family. Perhaps I feel close to you because I helped to keep you from drowning yesterday. I have spoken to the other members of the community. They feel as I do. There is no need to be afraid of us. Your fears are ours, as are your joys."

Mrs. Taylor smiled and set a plate of bacon, eggs, and muffins before Walker and Daniel.

Walker looked into her eyes. He could tell that she, too, knew that he was keeping a secret, one that he was afraid she would never understand. It might even turn her against him if he tried to explain.

Walker and Daniel ate quickly. From across the room Eunice crawled out of bed. She carried a rag doll to the table and sat in her place next to Walker.

"Good morning, Walker," she said, wiping the sleep from her eyes. "I think you will find your family today."

"What makes you think that?" Walker asked.

Eunice shrugged. "I do not know for sure. I dreamed you were standing with your parents in a big town with tall buildings. That is what I do not understand. Rochester is smaller than Stony Creek. You did say that you live in Rochester, right?"

"Yeah, sort of," Walker said.

"Well, where I saw you there were hundreds of other folks, too," she said.

"That's a strange dream all right," Walker said.

Outside a horse whinnied and a buggy rolled to a halt at the Taylor's door.

"That is Nathaniel," Lemuel said. "Are you boys ready?"

Walker crammed the last bit of bacon onto his fork and stuffed it in his mouth.

"That was a great breakfast, Mrs. Taylor," Walker said.

"All set?" Daniel asked, moving toward the door.

"You bet," Walker said, glancing at Eunice. She was still staring at him as though he hadn't even begun to answer all her questions.

"'Bye, Mrs. Taylor, and thank you." Walker said it as though it might be forever–as though Eunice's dream might come true. But suddenly he wasn't sure that he wanted it to be.

Chapter 10

❧ *Rochester* ☙

The sun hadn't peeked over the horizon when Walker saw four men aboard a horse-drawn wagon in front of the Taylor cabin. In the grey predawn light a warm mist hovered over the ground, giving the entire setting a ghostly appearance.

"Good morning, Lemuel. . .Daniel," a man in his early thirties said from the front of the wagon. He watched the three new riders climb aboard. "We have not met, Walker, but I have heard much about you. My name is Nathaniel Millerd. I am Daniel's brother-in-law. Please call me Nate."

"Uh, thanks, Mr. Millerd, er, Nate," Walker said, taking the powerful grip of the man before him. Walker had heard a lot about Nathaniel Millerd, too, but it was not idle chitchat. It was from the glowing words written about him in Michigan history books. It was from tales told in Mr. Dillon's lectures. It was from museum people and re-enactors who spoke in reverent tones about how important Nathaniel Millerd was, not only to Stony Creek, but to Oakland County and all of Michigan.

Nate's blue eyes, eager face, and playful smile put Walker at ease. He wasn't at all like the old stern-faced man whose photograph hung on the museum wall—and for good reason. A camera that could record people's faces would not be invented for another forty years! In fact, all of the people sitting on the wagon with Walker would either be dead or very old men by the time the first tintype was made. Their faces would be haggard and drawn from the years of struggle on the frontier. Even Daniel would be in his fifties before his first pictures would be etched onto the primitive metal plates.

Walker took a seat on the flatbed dray alongside three other men. It was the same sort of rig Walker had ridden with his Hart Middle friends for hayrides. This wagon, however, was pulled by two real horses, not by a fifty horsepower tractor.

"I am Elisha," the man next to Walker said. He smiled as he offered his right hand to Walker.

"I am Joshua," the next added. Walker shook his hand.

"And I am Lemuel Junior," the third said. "I am the eldest of Daniel's brothers. We are glad to have you with us, Walker."

There was a look of calm in each of their faces that gave Walker a warm feeling. He really was welcome, like a long lost member of the family which in every way he was.

"Get along, Clementine," Nate Millerd said, snapping the whip over the lead horse's head.

The wagon moved down the hill toward the creek barely sixty feet from where Walker had been fishing just the day before. At the river's edge the horses waded in. The rushing stream came up to the hubs of the wheels, and Walker lifted his bare feet to avoid the chilly water. The horses followed a narrow lane up a gradual rise. There was a hill on the right and an acre of flat land on the left.

Walker stared at the level area. It looked strangely familiar. What's wrong with this picture? he wondered. I know! That's where the old graveyard should be! His eyes searched the landscape. But there's no sign of it— no wrought iron fence, no tall tombstones.

Suddenly Walker understood. Of course not! The first people who died at Stony Creek are riding in the wagon with me right now—Nathaniel Millerd, Reverend Taylor, Elisha, Joshua, Lemuel Junior. Even Daniel. I know where every one of their gravestones are.

A creepy feeling swept over Walker. The hairs prickled on the back of his neck as he looked at the faces of the men who chatted and laughed amongst themselves as the wagon rambled along the bumpy trail. In a few years all of them will be dead, thought Walker. Maybe I will be buried here, too. Thin, grey, almost unreadable marble stones will be all that is left to show that they—we—ever existed. A frog welled up so big in Walker's throat that he could barely swallow.

"What is wrong, Walker?" Daniel asked. "You look as if you have seen a ghost."

Walker wanted to explain his eerie sensation—his premonition which was more like a "post-monition". He knew it would happen. For him it was ancient history. The only thing that he wasn't sure of was whether he would be part of the graveyard setting. Instead he just turned his face away from Daniel and watched the horses pull the wagon to the top of the hill.

As they crested the knoll, Walker thought about the dream Eunice had told him about, the one where she had seen him on the streets of Rochester. She could not have possibly envisioned the town as she did. But he knew from her description that she had seen it as it would one day be. Maybe her dream had taken her forward in time, just as he had gone back in time in real life. It was too strange.

As he stared ahead Walker expected to see St. Paul's steeple rise out of the woods. But it didn't. Neither did the two-story apartment building where he had delivered a prescription on his bike the day before last. He saw only the woods on his left, the swamp on his right, and the trail in front of him.

The wagon soon crossed a path that cut off to the left behind them. That must be Parkdale Road, Walker thought. He looked down it hoping to see the blue water tank with the name Rochester written in big black letters. It was not to be seen, nor would it even be built for another hundred years. Walker began to lose hope. How was he ever going to get home?

The wagon continued past a log cabin and a few shanties. The horses angled to the left and approached a tall, unpainted wood building on the bank of a narrow, fast-flowing stream. Nathaniel pulled on the reins and called, "Whoa."

Whoa? Walker thought. Whoa, what? This isn't Rochester. It's nothing. No Main Street, no stores, no churches, no people. What would he be whoa-ing for? Then it struck him. The creek. The tall, odd-shaped building. This is Hersey Mill, the first business in town. I'm on Main Street right now! Lipuma's Coney Island should be right here, and the Paint Creek Tavern there. A hundred yards ahead should be University and Main, the busiest corner in Rochester.

Not a soul was in sight. Walker remembered how only yesterday he had almost been creamed by a guy in an old Chevy who ran the red light. Today the problem won't be the traffic thought Walker. It will be finding the intersection at all.

The horses stopped. All the men hopped off the wagon and walked to the mill. On one side was the river and on the other was the millrace. Walker was the last to go inside. His eyes were drawn to the cogs and wheels and wide leather belts that whirled throughout the vast room. Everything seemed to be connected to something else as if he were inside a gigantic Pentium processor, like in the movie *Tron*.

And it was loud. Not heavy metal, rock concert loud, but loud enough so you couldn't hear a thing anyone said.

Walker smelled the sweet, heavily oiled leather straps that drove the wooden cogs. His eyes were seized by the whirling gears. His ears pounded from the rumbling of the grinding wheels. He tasted the wheat dust that clouded the air and tickled his nose. His bare feet pulsed from the plank floor vibrating riotously beneath him.

John Hersey sat at his roll-top desk. Next to him was the stone grinding wheel that was crushing grains of wheat as they dropped in a steady stream from a bin high above his head. He stood when he saw the seven Taylor men coming through his door.

Mr. Hersey pulled a long wooden handle that stuck up from the floor beside him. The flow of grain ceased. He yanked another lever and the crushing stone came to a halt. The noise level dropped from deafening to a dull roar. Mr. Hersey approached the wooden counter where Lemuel Taylor stood.

"How can I help you, Lem?" John Hersey asked.

"We need eight sacks of flour, Jack," Mr. Taylor said. "Two each of buckwheat, cornmeal, farina, and rye."

Walker listened as Mr. Taylor and Mr. Hersey settled on the price of the flour. Soon Nate lifted a twenty pound sack of buckwheat onto Walker's left shoulder. Walker followed the Taylors outside to the wagon and tossed his bag on top of the others.

Everyone climbed aboard, and Nate Millerd cracked the whip over Clementine's head. The wagon proceeded along the narrow trail that would one day be Main Street. Walker glanced eagerly to each side hoping to see something that he recognized—his dad's store, Red Knapp's, Home Bakery, anything at all. Instead the wagon rolled along the dusty path until it came to another building that looked like Hersey's mill.

Again Nate brought the horses to a halt, and the entire Taylor band went inside. The noise here was worse than at the gristmill.

Walker looked toward the far end of the building and saw logs coming down the river. Water flowed through a millrace and turned a set of cogs. Men stationed along the way used long poles to channel tree trunks three feet across and twenty feet long down the river through a narrow chute. A ten-foot-long saw blade slashed up and down through the logs. Walker stood in awe at how close the men worked to the enormous blade. One slip and a man could lose a hand—or his life—in an instant.

Inch-thick boards came out at the end of the mill, some of them a foot wide and twenty feet long. Men in one area loaded planks onto wagons, while others stacked theirs into squares for drying.

"My father is ordering a load of lumber for our own

flour mill," Daniel said. "They will bring it out to us this afternoon."

When Mr. Taylor finished talking to the man at the desk, everyone followed him to the wagon.

Nate directed the horses farther south to a narrow wooden bridge. As they crossed it Walker looked down at a stream which ran fast and deep enough to swamp a wagon and drown horses. This must be the Clinton River, he thought. We've gone the whole length of Rochester and all we've seen are two mills. A sinking feeling came over him as he realized he wasn't going to find his parents today, and probably not any time soon.

Chapter 11

🦢 *The Mail* 🦢

They traveled another quarter of a mile before Nate stopped at an ornate, two-story, white frame house. It was the first permanent-looking home Walker had seen. Everyone went up the stairs onto a wide porch. Mr. Taylor knocked on the door and soon shook hands with the man who answered. Walker and Daniel were the last to go inside and found the others already talking to a man wearing a visor and arm garters, white shirt, black trousers, and black string tie.

"It is good that you came when you did," Dr. Chipman, the postmaster, was saying. "The stagecoach just arrived. I will sort your mail right away. The new corduroy road from Detroit to Royal Oak washed out in several places, so the weekly postal wagon was late. Today the teamster told me that a pack of wolves spooked his horses about two miles south of here and nearly turned his wagon. He drove the wolves away with a blast from his shotgun."

"We can wait," Nathaniel Millerd said. "The rest of our errands are done. We will be outside." He turned and led the others to the door.

The Stony Creek men went to the front yard and sat in the shade of two large chestnut trees. Walker joined them, sitting alongside Daniel.

"I understand your family may live nearby," Nate Millerd said, glancing at Walker. "Did you want to look for them while we are here?"

Walker scanned the unfamiliar landscape. "No," he said, shaking his head. "They're not here."

"You sound so certain," Nate said. "I thought you may have become lost along the river, and that is how you came to our village. Your family is probably searching for you right now."

"Not a chance," Walker said with a sigh. "I'll be ready to go back to Stony Creek when you are."

"The mail will be ready in a few minutes," Nathaniel said. "We will leave as soon as it is."

Walker climbed onto the wagon and layed his head on a flour sack. He gazed into the clear blue sky while the other men stood in front of the house. A few minutes later Lemuel Taylor came out with several small bundles and envelopes. On top was a copy of the *Detroit Gazette*. Soon the wagon was heading north through "town."

Daniel joined Walker and stretched out in the back of the wagon. The two boys looked up into the sky as the wagon bounced back across the Clinton River Bridge.

"Not what you were hoping for, I take it," Daniel

whispered.

"No," Walker said, swallowing hard. "I guess I'd just better make the best of it. One thing for sure is that I couldn't be making up everything I know about the twenty-first century. I also know that you're right. If I try to tell people about when I'm from, they'll all think I'm a loony toon."

"A loony toon?" Daniel asked.

"Yeah, you know, like Daffy Duck or Bugs Bunny, the cartoon char . . ." Walker hesitated. "There I go again, using words from my own time. It's just that so many of them are so old that I forget they haven't been around forever. But if I'm not careful, no one will listen to anything I say."

"I will not argue with that," Daniel said. "But if it makes you feel better, I do believe you."

"Sure you do. You're a kid," Walker said. "We're both kids. But grown-ups who have been tricked by strangers before won't believe me. Not for a minute. Even if, by some miracle I could prove that I was from 2002, they'd probably burn me at the stake for being a witch."

"We do not do that much anymore," Daniel said with a hint of a smile. "At least not us Baptists. We just tar and feather people and run them out of town."

"Oh, well then, I guess that would be okay," Walker said, returning Daniel's smile.

"What else are you afraid to tell?" Daniel asked.

"Everything. Look over there," Walker said pointing to a large maple tree. "My dad's drug store should be right about there, as near as I can make out. This whole trail," he waved his hand out into the distance, "this will be Main Street. It will be lined with bike shops, restaurants, dry cleaners, brew pubs, jewelers, book-sellers, realtors, department stores, travel agencies, art galleries, antique dealers, ice cream parlors, doctors and lawyers offices. Everything you'd ever want would be on one side of the street or the other. If we stood here for more than two seconds in my time, we'd be flattened by a forty ton gravel truck thundering through town at about thirty-five miles an hour." Walker stopped and took a breath. He looked over at Daniel whose eyes were wide in amazement.

"The only trees you'd see," Walker continued, "would be a row planted for decoration fifteen years ago, and I don't mean 1809. I mean 1987. Everything would be neat and clean. There would be nothing but brick, glass, and cement everywhere. There wouldn't be enough dirt along here to grow a blade of grass, not that anyone would, but it just gives you an idea of how things are, or were, or will be. Oh, I don't know. I just know I'm not supposed to be here, at least not now."

"That is where you are wrong, Walker," Daniel said firmly. "I think you are supposed to be here—now."

"Why in the world should I be here in 1824?" Walker asked with a touch of hopelessness in his voice.

"Maybe you came here to stop something from happening," Daniel said, "or to learn something that people in your time have forgotten. Maybe you are here to show us something."

"But why me? I'm just a kid," Walker said.

"Someone older might not be able to do whatever it is you are supposed to do," Daniel said. "Look, Walker, I do not know any more about this than you, but you must be here for a very good reason."

"Well, whatever it is," Walker said, "I think we'd better keep quiet about it. Even though your parents and the others suspect something is going on, I'd still better not tell them that I'm from twenty-oh-two."

"You are right about that, Walker," Daniel said. "Remember what I told you about Baptists not burning witches? After hearing what you just told me, they might make an exception in your case." He smiled and gave Walker a wink.

"Oh, thanks," Walker said. "You're a real comfort."

"Just joking," said Daniel. "But we had best bide our time. If you are here for a reason, whatever it is, it will happen sooner or later. Until then, you can count on me to keep your secret—and be your friend."

"Thanks," Walker said. "My dad says that one good friend is as many as some people get in a lifetime. For this lifetime, I'm glad I've found you."

Chapter 12

ꕥ *"Home"* ꕥ

Judging by where the sun was in the sky and by the gnawing hunger in his stomach, Walker guessed it was about noon. Nathaniel Millerd drove the wagon past the gristmill on Paint Creek. He then led the horses to the right. Walker knew this would one day be every kid's favorite corner in town because the Dairy Queen would be here. Even though nothing was there but trees, bushes, and a log cabin, it didn't stop Walker from thinking about being next in line at his favorite fast food place. Man, could I go for a couple of dogs and a DQ Blizzard, Walker thought.

He was sure he wasn't crazy, but Walker knew he couldn't explain what was going on, either. It was all too strange even to sort out for himself, much less convince an adult. If Daniel was right and he was there for a purpose, it would be nice to have some idea what it was that would take him back to his own time.

One thing was sure. Unless he could find his way home soon, he wouldn't have to worry about school for the rest of this year. He could forget about his history exam and memorizing all those worthless dates and names. Not that it wouldn't be nice to know more about early Michigan right now.

Walker began to wonder how his knowledge of the future might help him. He was pretty sure he couldn't change anything major, like inventing the telephone or the light bulb. As common as they were in his time, he had no idea how they were made. But maybe he could take advantage of some of the history that he did remember.

Walker looked at the newspaper that Mr. Taylor was reading. It was the *Detroit Gazette*, May 18, 1824. One of the headlines read, "Dr. Beaumont treats man with gunshot wound on Mackinac Island. Learns secrets to digestion." News must travel slow in the 1800s, Walker thought. That happened in 1822. Mr. Dillon told us about it in class last week. Another headline read, "Erie Canal nears completion. Eastern pioneers plan for spring '25 journey to Michigan Territory." Well, that much is true, at least according to Daniel. Toward the bottom of the front page, a third headline caught Walker's eye. "Lewis Cass begins platting local towns."

Lewis Cass? Walker thought. I've heard about him. He was the man Cass City, Cassopolis, Cass River, Cass County, and who knows how many other places were named for. And he did plat Rochester. Dad told me that a hundred times. If he hadn't planned Rochester like he did, it probably wouldn't have made it into the 20th century, let alone the 21st. He was probably the most important person, other than Mickey Lolich or Madonna, to ever set foot in Rochester.

Walker decided right then that he was going to try to meet Governor Cass. That might be why I'm here, he thought. Maybe I'm supposed to help him do something. I'd better stay on the good side of Mr. Taylor, he thought as the wagon bumped along the rutted road toward Stony Creek. If he thinks I'm crazy, he will never let me get close to Governor Cass.

Soon Nathaniel Millerd guided the horses back through the gurgling Stony Creek waters and into the small community. Walker looked around him at all the log cabins and barns. Stony Creek was a city compared to Rochester. He thought about how he had helped build Lemuel Taylor's gristmill the day before. Maybe I've been sent here to do something like that. Mr. Taylor said he couldn't have done it without me. I may have already changed history. If I hadn't been here to help with the corner posts and setting the millstone, maybe the people of Stony Creek would not have had enough flour to live through the winter. Walker's spirits brightened. I may wake up tomorrow in my own bed, and all this will be like a long strange dream.

Walker looked to his right. The land was not yet cleared of the brush and trees that he knew would one day be the pasture for the best herd of Holstein cattle in the state.

Eventually, when it was no longer a working farm

and the museum had become a place for historic shows, that same meadow would be the location for Civil War battle reenactments. Real cannons would boom sixteen-pound iron balls a couple hundred yards, knocking targets to smithereens. Foot soldiers would shoot and reload their muskets and rifles. Cavalries would charge enemy brigades. Men pretending to be shot and killed would be strewn all over the place. Later, they would rise like so many heroic ghosts and join the others in lively debates of war tactics while washing away the gun powder and fake blood. They would talk about the real Civil War battles that happened hundreds of miles away and had casualties of a much more permanent nature.

Reenactments were always the best part of coming here for Walker. Indians would camp in wigwams along the stream as they once had. Sam Morrison, Walker's dad, would dress up as Lemuel Taylor and tell groups of people why he had brought his family from New York to Michigan Territory. Walker could watch all this without ever doing anything. If he got bored, he could simply hop on his bike and go home to his air-conditioned house and relax in front of the TV.

The wagon rolled to a stop outside the Taylor log cabin. Walker's day-dreaming was interrupted by Elisha Taylor, who held a burlap bag at the edge of the wagon. "I need a hand here, Walker." Elisha hoisted a sack of flour onto Walker's shoulder, and Walker turned to go inside.

As he walked along, Walker heard Nathaniel Millerd talking to Joshua. "Did you see that Indian off to the side of the road back there?" Nate said.

"I saw him, all right," Joshua said. "That was Wa-se-gah. He is the one Harry saved from burning to death three months ago. Wa-se-gah was at a tribal ceremony and fell into the bonfire. His friends pulled him out and rushed him here for Harry to take care of. Harry had to amputate his left leg, or Wa-se-gah would have died that night."

"Well, I did not like the look he gave us as we went by," Nathaniel said. "He just sat there, half hiding his face but glancing at us with an angry sneer. You would think he'd be a little more grateful since one of us saved his life."

"Harry told me that if there is one thing he learned since becoming a doctor," Joshua said, "it is that you cannot predict what sick people might do—whether they are red, white, yellow, or brown. Their illness gets to them and they behave differently than they normally would."

"Maybe we should watch for him tonight," Nathaniel said.

Walker stood next to the wagon listening to the two older Taylor brothers talk. He remembered the story the museum people often told about how Harry Taylor saved an Indian by amputating his burned leg, and that three months later the Indian came to Stony Creek to kill Harry. The Indian had banged on Elisha Taylor's door, thinking Elisha was Harry. He wanted to kill Harry because, with only one leg he could no longer do the work of a brave. To him that was a fate worse than death.

This may be why I'm here, Walker thought. This is an important event in Stony Creek's history. It could be that this is how I earn my way back to 2002. Perhaps I'm the one who saves Elisha's life.

Walker carried the flour sack into the cabin and set it on the dirt floor. Mrs. Taylor and Eunice were carrying the boiled venison, bread, and potatoes from the fireplace to the table for the midday meal.

Walker turned and saw Mr. Taylor set his loaded musket in its place above the cabin door. I may have to use that tonight, Walker thought. This could get me home.

Chapter 13

❧ *The Encounter* ☙

Walker ate lunch sitting in the chair between Daniel and Eunice and across from Mr. and Mrs. Taylor. It was early in the afternoon and he began to think that the rest of the day might get very busy. Stony Creek was fighting for its life just as the museum people had said. To earn his keep, Walker would have to work hard also. Still, if tonight was to be the clash between Wa-se-gah and Elisha, Walker might have to stay awake and be alert enough to save Elisha's life. He could not drain himself as he had the day before.

After finishing lunch Walker carried a sack of nails down to the river. He was starting to realize that the mill was even more important to the Stony Creek people than their own homes. The cabins were needed as day-to-day shelters, but the mill was their lifeblood—the source of their food, their income, their future.

In the distance Walker saw two horses coming over the hill pulling a wagon piled high with lumber. Walker's job was to help unload the boards and nail at least some of them into place.

After they all unloaded the lumber, Elisha and Mr.

Taylor measured and sawed the planks. They stayed about one board ahead of Daniel and Walker who nailed the boards to the mill's frame. Board after board went into place as the afternoon wore on. Finally Mrs. Taylor clanged the dinner bell. Mr. Taylor called over to Daniel, "Time to eat."

Walker nearly fell on his face. Any thoughts of performing noble deeds to save anyone, including himself, had vanished by mid-afternoon. He wanted nothing more than food and sleep, not necessarily in that order.

Walker followed Daniel and Elisha who trailed their father to the house. Elisha entered his side of the double log cabin and Lemuel, Daniel, and Walker went into the elder Taylor's home. As tired as Walker was, the aroma of food in the crude fireplace jolted him to alertness. Why does everything smell so good? he wondered.

Lemuel's prayer lasted forever. Walker turned his eyes from his folded hands to the steaming platter in the middle of the table. Slowly he moved his left hand to the fork in front of him without actually touching it. He set his sights on the largest, juiciest piece of meat on the platter. The instant Lemuel says amen, Walker thought, that huge hunk of hog will be safely on my plate.

Just at that moment Walker felt a sharp sting on his butt. He jerked his head toward Daniel who had his eyes lowered reverently. But looking closer Walker noticed a tiny smile dancing in the corners of his friend's mouth. Behind his back Daniel clasped a two pronged serving fork. Walker withdrew his hand from the table and tried not to think about how starved he was. How much longer would Reverend Taylor go on?

Finally Mr. Taylor said amen. This time, Walker's amen was right on cue. His hand shot to his fork and then to the platter. The trophy portion of pork was his. It was his turn to smirk at Daniel who had not quite managed to get the serving fork from around his back in time to snag the prized piece of meat.

Walker ate like he had never eaten before. Between bites everyone talked about events of that day. Walker's last bit of energy was spent devouring two large portions of rhubarb cobbler. It was a dessert he had never much cared for in his old life, but now he attacked it with great enthusiasm.

Soon after eating the boys made their way to the loft. Walker stripped down and settled himself on the linsey-woolsey sheets that covered the corn husk mattress. He was hot and tired, but he knew he had to stay alert for the one-legged Indian. His eyes drooped as the humming of the crickets droned in the nearby woods. The darkness of night and the surrounding wilderness seemed to close in around the Taylor cabin.

Two hours passed. Walker heard a night owl hoot in the distance. He was struggling to stay awake when he slowly became aware of the soft thumping of a drum. He bolted upright. Wa-se-gah, he thought. He's coming. The drumbeat became louder as the Indian drew nearer. Walker slipped silently from his cot and pulled his shirt and pants on. He stepped down the ladder and moved silently to Mr. Taylor's bed. He grasped Reverend Taylor's shoulder.

"Mr. Taylor," Walker whispered. "Wa-se-gah is coming. He is here to kill Elisha. Wa-se-gah thinks Elisha is Harry who cut off his leg three months ago. He wants revenge."

Just then Walker heard a loud pounding. It wasn't on Lemuel's door, but on Elisha's door directly across from it. Walker hurried from Mr. Taylor's bedside and listened as Wa-se-gah beat again at Elisha's entrance.

"Who is there?" Walker heard Elisha say.

"It is Wa-se-gah!" came the voice of the Indian. "Let me in or I will burn you out."

"What do you want?" Elisha asked.

"I have come to make you pay for cutting off my leg," the Indian growled. "I can do nothing but women's work. Now I will make you die."

Walker lifted Lemuel's musket from its place above the door. A firm voice spoke from behind. "That gun is for bears and wolves, Walker, not for men." It was Reverend Taylor. "I will try to make Wa-se-gah understand his mistake. Stand behind me should I fail."

"Yes, sir," Walker said, stepping back. The rusty hinge squeaked as Mr. Taylor opened the door.

Startled, Wa-se-gah spun around and faced Lemuel.

When he saw the Reverend was unarmed, he stepped forward raising a crude stone-headed hatchet over his head. Walker moved from the shadows and brought the gun into firing position. Just then Elisha opened his door. The Indian pivoted on his makeshift crutch to see Elisha pointing a musket at his head.

Dropping the hatchet to his side, Wa-se-gah grumbled, "I will get you one day." He turned and hobbled away.

Mr. Taylor turned from the door to face Walker. "This is very curious," he said, staring into Walker's eyes. "First I will thank you for warning me. But I must also ask how you knew this was going to happen? How could you possibly know that it was Wa-se-gah and that he had mistaken Elisha for Harry?"

Walker shuffled his feet. He felt trapped. Without giving up his secret, he could not explain that the story of Harry, Elisha, and the one-legged Indian had become legendary in Stony Creek history.

"J-just a hunch, I guess," Walker stammered.

Lemuel Taylor stared at Walker. His eyes softened and he seemed satisfied with Walker's feeble reply. "Well, your hunch may have saved Elisha's life," Lemuel Taylor said. "Perhaps mine, too. You are a very brave young man. You could have stayed in the loft until the whole thing was over and no one would have known that Wa-se-gah was even coming."

Walker's face burned with the praise of so great a

man as Lemuel Taylor, as well as knowing that he had almost blown his secret. That was too close. He would have to be more careful. He turned toward the ladder where Daniel was standing, rubbing his eyes.

"What is happening?" Daniel asked.

"I'll tell you upstairs," Walker whispered.

Everyone went back to bed and Walker explained to Daniel how close he had come to tripping himself up. He remained awake hoping that what he had done would get him back to 2002. Maybe I don't go right away, Walker thought. Maybe I'll just wake up tomorrow morning in my own bed like nothing happened.

He finally drifted off to sleep.

- - - - -

When he awakened, Walker was still in his narrow, lumpy bed. Daniel was standing next to him.

"Good morning, Mr. Hero," Daniel said with a smile."Whatever it is that you have to do to get yourself home must be pretty important. Let's have breakfast."

Chapter 14

✻ *June* ✻

As the days passed into weeks, Walker saw nothing new that might lead him back to his own time. The longer he was with the Taylors, the less he thought about home. And he didn't see any point in agonizing over something he couldn't do anything about.

As time went on Walker began to wonder if he really was from 2002. Memories of his old activities were dreamlike, while his day-to-day life in 1824 was as real as the callouses on his hands and the muscles in his arms. Some nights he would lie awake trying to remember the faces of his teachers and friends at Hart Middle. The images of his brothers, even his mom and dad, were becoming blurry.

Somewhere along the way Walker had begun to feel like a big brother to Daniel and Eunice as the three of them played and worked their summer days away. Walker considered Daniel not only a close friend, but a terrific brother. Several times Daniel had saved Walker from letting his secret slip out. Once when Nathaniel Millerd was saying how the wolves were killing all the sheep, Walker said "Really? I didn't think wolves had been seen around here for a hundred years or so . . ."

Just as Walker caught his own mistake, Daniel jumped in and changed the subject. "Oh, Nate," he said anxiously, "when is Governor Cass coming to plat Rochester?" Nathaniel, who was much more interested in political activities than farming problems, quickly forgot Walker's blunder.

Walker was also pleased with the neat tricks Daniel had shown him. He could make slide whistles out of green twigs and bubble pipes out of corn cobs. In fact the two boys had become closer in one month than Walker had ever been with any of his old friends—even Kenny Fisher, who had been his best buddy from the time they were toddlers.

It was the same with Eunice. Walker felt like her big brother, too. He learned all her little ways—the sweet, the annoying, and everything in between. He began to watch over her because she was always getting into dangerous situations trying to prove how tough she was. She would take any dare the Stony Creek boys could think of, or double-dare them when things got dull.

Once on a bet from Tommy Groesbeck, the blacksmith's ten-year-old son, she hopped into the billy goat's pen and teased it by tapping its nose with a long horse whip. When the goat decided that enough was enough, Eunice ran for the gate. Rushing to escape, she stepped barefoot into a large soft pile of goat manure.

It threw her off stride and she sprawled flat on her face ten feet from the fence. As she struggled to her feet the goat lowered its head and began a charge toward his tormentor's behind. Walker leaped into the pen just in time to steer the animal off course.

Eunice jumped to her feet and ran to safety through the gate. The goat seemed to have no real quarrel with Walker, who hopped back over the fence leaving the goat to glare at Eunice. Eunice told Tommy that it was his turn to get into the pen. Tommy took one look at the enraged goat and remembered his mother had told him that he had to weed the garden that morning.

Walker also saved Eunice from a two-hundred pound mother pig after Eunice had snatched one of the squealing babies from the pig pen. This adventure was also the result of a dare, this time by her cousin Covil. To Eunice's surprise the big sow outran her, something Walker would not have believed if he hadn't seen it. Once again Walker hopped the fence and raced to Eunice's rescue. He lowered his shoulder and dived into the side of the mother pig, much as he had done on Hart's football team to clear the way for a running back. Walker and the sow got up slowly, each a little stunned from the encounter. Eunice wisely dropped the baby pig and sprinted to safety.

Still, Eunice won more than her share of dares, especially when it came to riding Daisy, the Guernsey heifer which had developed the odd habit of jerking its head up when coming into the barn from pasture. No boy could stay aboard Daisy as long as Eunice could, nor delight in the experience as much as she.

It was now the middle of June. The sun was getting hotter and the days longer. The gristmill was nearly done. Walker and Daniel began to dig the canal for the millrace. Shoveling load after load of dirt was hard work. The whole millrace idea seemed stupid to Walker. After all, the river is right there. Why not use that water to turn the grinding wheel? It was Elisha who set Walker straight. They couldn't control the flow of the river, he said, because its depth changed too much during the year. In the spring surging currents would turn the wheel too fast. In the fall it might not turn it at all. With a narrow millrace they could channel the water they needed and turn the grinding wheel at a constant rate all year long.

That made just enough sense to keep Walker digging. Still, he wished he had a big gas-powered backhoe like construction workers had used to build the new high school across the road from Hart Middle. The whole millrace trench would take less than two hours with one of those babies, Walker reasoned.

Lemuel and Elisha were planning to build another mill about a quarter mile up the creek after the gristmill was done. This would be a sawmill to make boards for building new houses. The log cabins were too drafty and the roofs leaked. They were okay for the families' settling stage, but not as permanent homes.

When Walker wasn't helping with the mill, he spent his time with Daniel and Eunice tilling the fields. Daniel led the oxen while Walker rode the plow as it turned the soil. Eunice followed behind stabbing seeds into the moist black dirt. It was long hot work, especially for Walker who had never done any real labor in his life. Still, when the day was done he went to bed with a good feeling, proud of himself for helping his family and community. Instead of resting his head on a soft pillow at night without a clue as to how he might amuse himself the next day, he now had a very clear idea of what to expect—hot, hard work and lots of it. But it was always work that was important to everyone at Stony Creek.

Chapter 15

☙ *Grayling* ☙

"Race you to the mill," Walker challenged Daniel as the two stood waist-deep in the creek water. They were splashing each other and horsing around as they skinny-dipped to cool off after a hot day of digging the mill-race.

"You mean swim there?" Daniel asked.

"Yeah, of course. Unless you think you can walk," Walker said with a laugh.

"I do not swim," Daniel said.

"Really? Why not?" Walker was surprised.

"Never had a need to," Daniel answered.

"How could you live this close to water and not have a need to swim?" Walker asked.

"What good would it do?" Daniel said.

That stopped Walker. He thought about it and realized Daniel was right. Except for this small mill pond where the water was fifteen feet deep and thirty feet across, there was no place to swim. For the most part Stony Creek swept along only about waist deep.

Walker thought back to when he was seven years old. His mom made him take swimming lessons. If he didn't pass the course, he couldn't go fishing by himself at their cottage up north. He was so scrawny that it took him three months just to get from the "sink like a rock" beginner stage to the "paddle around like a scared dog" level at the YMCA pool.

Here at Stony Creek Daniel had no reason to go through all that. Mrs. Taylor had plenty of other dangers facing her family than to worry about a little water safety.

"I don't know, it cools you off," Walker said with a shrug.

"I can get just as wet in three feet of water as you can in ten," Daniel said. "Besides, I do not think anyone else in our village can swim either. Who would teach me?"

That took Walker by surprise. No one here can swim? How could that be? Then he remembered that he'd never actually seen his own father swim, nor his grandfather. Maybe kids never went swimming in the olden days, Walker thought. Maybe they just splashed around like they were doing now.

"Would you like to be able to do this?" Walker said. "Watch. I'll dive to the bottom and bring up a stone. Then I'll go to the mill and back using four different strokes."

Walker free-styled out to the middle, surface-dived, and disappeared toward the bottom. At about ten feet, he realized the pond was deeper than he had thought.

He turned and swam to the top. Then he backstroked to the mill, touched it, and returned starting with the breast stroke. He finally splashed up to Daniel doing the butterfly. "That might be a world record Individual Medley for 1824," Walker said with a laugh.

"Yes, that was pretty good," Daniel admitted. "Where is the stone?"

Walker shook the water from his hair. "It was too deep," Walker said. "I got close, but it felt like my ears were going to pop. I did that once diving for clams. My eardrums broke and I got really sick. I threw up for about a whole day, but that was probably because I ate the clams. Anyway, would you like to learn how to swim? It's easy."

"Naw," Daniel said. "Let's go fishing instead."

"Fine by me," Walker said as he followed Daniel out of the creek. They retrieved their clothes from the branches of a wild raspberry bush. "I love to fish. What do you usually catch?"

"Grayling, mainly," Daniel said, picking up his shirt. "But I get some pike and trout now and then."

"Grayling?" Walker said. "I never heard of a fish by that name. Is it spelled like the town up north?"

"I don't know about any town up north, but the grayling fish are great fighters. They have a tall fin that runs the length of their back. When you hook a grayling, it flies right out of the water."

"Really? That sounds like the fish I had on my line

the day I came here," Walker said, looking puzzled. "Blunt nose and shaped like a torpedo, right?"

"Torpedo?" Daniel asked.

"Yeah, uh, like a big bullet," Walker said, shaking his head. He'd done it again. "What do you catch them on?"

"Bees," Daniel said, pulling his shirt over his head.

"Bees?" Walker asked. He buttoned his pants and stared at Daniel in wonder. "You mean live bees?"

"Sure," Daniel said with a shrug.

"You catch fish using live bees for bait," Walker repeated, making sure he had heard Daniel correctly.

Daniel nodded like it was no big deal.

"How do you put live bees on a hook without getting stung?" Walker asked.

"Carefully," Daniel said. He flashed a knowing smile to his friend. He waited for Walker to pull his shirt on and then started for the log cabin. "Come on. I will show you."

Daniel ran inside and grabbed a wooden box that had a leather bellows on one side and a tin spout sticking out the other. He dipped a rag in some pork grease and stuck it in the box. Then he picked up a water bucket and lid. He placed a wide-brimmed straw hat on his head and put on a pair of thick leather gloves. Next he threw a thin mesh cloth over his shoulders and headed out the door.

Walker followed Daniel about thirty yards into the

woods. Daniel stopped near a tree that looked as if it were about to fall over. He removed a pouch from around his neck and took two stones from inside. Then he knelt on the ground and struck the stones together. Sparks shot onto some dry leaves he had arranged in a cup. After the leaves burst into a flame Daniel stuffed the cup into the smoker box. He worked the bellows, and soon big puffs of grey smoke came out of the funnel.

Daniel carried the smoking box to the old tree. By now Walker could see dozens of wild honey bees coming and going from a large hole in the trunk about four feet from the ground. Daniel put the mesh cloth over his hat to cover his head and squeezed several puffs of smoke into the hole. At first the bees swarmed all around him, but before long fewer bees were coming out of the tree. He reached in with his gloved hand and pulled out a thick comb of honey with bees crawling all over it. He jammed the whole mess into the pail, slapped the lid on, and ran back to the cabin.

Walker followed close at his heels.

When they got to the Taylor's house, Daniel stood outside the door and aimed the smoker nozzle into the box. He gave the bees several puffs and lifted the lid, brushing the bees into the pail. He then set the honeycomb, dripping with dark brown honey, onto a plate and took it into the kitchen.

"That will be for later," Daniel said, coming back outside. "Now we will catch some grayling."

Daniel grabbed a long wooden switch that had been leaning against the log cabin. It was already rigged with a string and hook. He picked up the pail of bees, the smoker, one glove, and a cord stringer. "Come with me," Daniel said as he started down the hill to the creek.

Walker followed Daniel to a wide place in the river behind Nate Millerd's cabin. He set the pail down and put his glove on.

"We will take turns," Daniel said. "First you hold the pole while I bait the hook."

Daniel smoked the bees once more before reaching his gloved hand inside the pail. He brought his hand out and slapped the lid back on. Between his thumb and second finger he held one slightly stunned honey bee. He took the line in the other hand and slipped the bee carefully onto the tiny, curved hook in such a way that the bee was still capable of flight.

Daniel waved the pole in the direction of the stream. The bee landed on the water. It remained for a moment airing its wings and then flew up about six inches.

In the next moment Walker saw a flash of silver and black streaking across the bottom of the stream. It exploded out of the water directly beneath the bee, its mouth gaping open.

Wham! The fish hit Daniel's hook and flew another two feet into the air. It looked like the same one Walker had on his dad's fly rod the day he arrived in the nineteenth century. It was spectacular.

The fish peaked in its flight, turned in midair, and shot back under the surface, with the hook firmly caught in his lower lip. It then slashed from one side of the stream to the other. Daniel held the long pole with both hands, giving the fish as much room as he could in order to tire it out.

Walker had never seen anyone catch such a large fish without a rod and reel. Finally Daniel brought it to the bank and pulled it ashore. The fish flopped around for a moment before Daniel grabbed it and slid it onto the stringer. Walker guessed it was about twenty inches long.

"That is a grayling," Daniel said with a triumphant grin. "Now it is your turn." He handed the pole to Walker, and the two made their way back to the bait box. Walker put on the glove and squeezed the smoker into the bucket of bees. He pulled one out, impaled it on the hook, and hurried back to the stream.

Over the next half hour Walker and Daniel landed three more grayling. Walker hadn't had so much fun fishing ever, and that included several deep sea trips with his brothers in Florida.

"That is enough for a meal," Daniel said after Walker had landed the fourth grayling. He lifted the heavy stringer, and Walker followed him to the cabin where Daniel got a knife. The two cleaned the fish for dinner.

Mrs. Taylor had made some good meals, but none could compare to this one. It was unforgettable in any time.

Chapter 16

❧ *Governor Cass* ☙

That night Walker dreamed of grayling and hot biscuits dripping with dark honey. In the morning he awakened to doves cooing on the roof just inches above his head. In the distance Stony Creek gurgled softly through the frontier community. Walker opened his eyes and saw Daniel holding some new clothes.

"Mother made these for you," Daniel said. "My father wants us to dress up for our meeting with Governor Cass in Rochester today. Mr. Cass is planning the streets there, and my father wants to talk to him about doing the same thing here."

Walker had forgotten all about the great statesman coming to Rochester and that he might learn or do something to earn his way back to 2002. Walker sat on the side of his bed for a moment before putting on his new blue-and-tan checked shirt and white trousers. He began to think how much he had changed in the past several weeks. He looked at his hands. Soft and smooth only a month before, they now were calloused and rough from shoveling, hoeing, and using frontier tools. He squeezed them into fists. His wrists had doubled in size. His fingers were strong like Lemuel's. His fingernails were worn down to nubs. Dirt and grit were forced under them. Walker knew his mom would have a major hissy if she saw how grimy they were.

Walker's old morning ritual of showering and shampooing before putting on fresh clean clothes had changed, too. He now climbed into the same pants and shirt he had pulled off the night before as he had collapsed into bed. If it had rained the previous day there would be mud caked on the knees, or plenty of thick brown dust if it hadn't.

Walker pulled his new clothes on and slid down the ladder. Mrs. Taylor was putting breakfast on the table. Mr. Taylor was wearing his black preaching suit, white shirt, and black string tie to meet with Governor Cass.

As Walker sat next to Daniel at his place at the table, a strange thought occurred to him. At his old home, the one on Fourth Street in the twenty-first century, Walker had never had a "place at the table." His mom always seemed to get the one closest to the stove, but other than that his dad and brothers sat in whatever chair happened to be available. The one with the best view of the TV, of course, would be taken first.

As he thought about it, Walker couldn't even remember when all of his family had gotten up in the morning and eaten breakfast together. During the school year he and his brothers attended different schools that started at different times. So each of his brothers would wait until the last possible second to hit the shower, devour a bowl of cereal, and fly out the door. Sometimes they didn't see each other for days in a row, much less sit at a particular place at the kitchen table for breakfast.

Walker's family never had dinner or went to bed at the same time, either. If it wasn't for church on Sundays, he might not see some of them at all.

Walker finished his ham and eggs and carried his plate to the wooden sink. He dipped some water from the bucket and rinsed it clean.

Mr. Taylor went to the barn and hitched the horses for the ride into town. Walker and Daniel hopped onto the wagon with Nate Millerd, Mr. Taylor and his older sons, Lemuel Junior, Elisha, and Joshua. The Stony Creek group travelled along the narrow trail and across the creek toward Rochester. They passed the two Rochester mills and crossed the wooden bridge at the Clinton River. Mr. Taylor brought the horses to a halt at Doctor Chipman's home.

Several carriages were there, some of them fancy ones. This must be the place, Walker thought as he jumped off the buggy. Inside they saw many well-dressed men standing around a large table. Maps, either rolled or flattened, lay all over it. Walker looked closely at the one spread out in the center of the table. He immediately realized that these men were planning the streets of Rochester!

Walker stood with Daniel in the background as Dr. Chipman introduced Lemuel Taylor to Governor Cass.

"Yes, I have heard much about you, Reverend Taylor," Lewis Cass said. "Your Stony Creek Village has become a major population center. You seem to be doing very well on your own."

"Thank you, Governor," Lemuel Taylor said. "The Lord has provided us with fertile land and favorable weather these first two summers. But we have come to ask your advice on planning the future of our small community. First, I would like you to meet my sons."

Lemuel Taylor began with Lemuel, Jr. and worked his way down to Daniel, saying something about each as the governor shook his hand. Walker gradually moved himself out of the way. He was startled when Mr. Taylor raised his voice and said, "and this is Walker Morrison, Governor Cass. He has become a valuable member of our community. Walker, I would like you to meet Governor Lewis Cass."

"Very glad to meet you, sir," Walker said nervously. "I've read a lot about you . . .," Walker stopped short of adding, ". . . in my history books."

After the introductions Mr. Cass turned to the surveyors. "Well, I believe we are done here. Let us go outside now and speak with Mr. Taylor about Stony Creek."

Maybe this is why I'm here, Walker thought. Maybe there is something on the map that is wrong and needs to be changed.

Walker looked over the shoulders of the men who had been making all the pencil marks on the village map. Three winding lines showed Stony Creek, Paint Creek, and Clinton River passing through the village. There was a small area marked "cemetery" where Walker knew Mount Avon was located. Another section was marked "School" where the board of education offices were. Several crisscrossing lines had street names. Trees—Walnut, Pine, Oak, and Elm were vertical lines, while First through Seventh were given to the horizontal ones. There's a mistake, Walker thought. Where "University" should be, the name "Fifth" is marked. Then he realized that the street probably was known as Fifth until Oakland University was built. Changing that on the map wouldn't alter history enough to earn him his way back to 2002, he decided.

Walker checked the rest of the map. Whoa, look at this! he thought. This is a big one. Main Street is marked to be only sixty feet wide. Walker knew for a fact that it was a hundred. He'd heard his dad say that if Lewis Cass hadn't made Main Street one hundred feet wide, Rochester would have died like so many other towns with narrow main streets. They just couldn't survive with all the twentieth century car and truck traffic. Lewis Cass seemed to know that downtown streets would one day need to be wider if the town was to prosper. Walker's dad had called it "vision."

Walker had to do something. This mistake was very

important. Either Governor Cass hadn't noticed it, or he didn't have as much vision as he was given credit for.

As Mr. Cass, his surveyors, and the Taylor men began to file out of Dr. Chipman's house, Walker stayed behind. He spotted a pencil and an eraser in the center of the table. He bent over pretending to redo one of his pants buttons while the last of the men stepped outside.

When no one was watching, Walker took the eraser and rubbed out the "60" in the middle of Main Street. He grabbed the pencil and, with a shaking hand, marked "100" in its place.

Beads of nervous sweat popped from his brow as he stepped back to make sure the change looked okay. He brushed some of the eraser marks off the map and hurried outside to join Daniel in the buggy.

"What is wrong?" Daniel whispered, seeing the anxious look on Walker's face.

"Can't tell you right now," Walker said. "But I may have just earned my way home."

Chapter 17

❧ *The Future* ❧

That night Daniel and Walker sat with the Stony Creek men who had gathered in Lemuel Taylor's cabin to talk about the meeting with Governor Cass. Nathaniel Millerd felt Mr. Cass should plan Stony Creek's streets as he had Rochester's.

"I am not so sure of that," Lemuel Taylor said. "Our village does not have to become a large town. One reason we moved from Aurelius was that it was too crowded. I think Stony Creek can be small and still suit all our people's needs."

"If a town does not grow, will it not eventually die?" Nathaniel said. "Stony Creek may one day lose out to a more aggressive village. Even Rochester, as small and far away as it is now, might expand and take over Stony Creek."

The men talked for hours, but finally Walker and Daniel went up the ladder to bed. Walker felt certain that by changing Governor Cass's plat map of Rochester, he was going to awaken in his own room, in his own house, in his own century. He was sure the only reason he had come to 1824 was to make Main Street one hundred feet wide.

As excited as Walker was to go home, he was also saddened by the thought of leaving the Taylors, especially Daniel. He lifted the blanket and crawled onto his lumpy mattress. I might miss Daniel, but I won't miss this bed, he thought.

The small candle flickered on the table between Daniel and Walker. Walker whispered to his friend, "If I'm not here tomorrow morning, it's because I've gone back to my own time."

"What makes you think that?" Daniel asked.

"I did something pretty important today," Walker said, "something that everyone gave Governor Cass credit for, but he really didn't do. I did it, and I had to come all the way from the twenty-first century to do it."

Walker couldn't help but smirk at the irony of it all. Lewis Cass wasn't such a hotshot. Walker began to think of all the Michigan names that might be given in his honor like Cass had gotten. Morrison Lake. Morrison Tech. Morrison County. He could even picture the poor band kids at Morrisonopolis High School not having enough time to spell the team's name on the football field at halftime. And the cheerleaders. "Give me an *M*. *M*. Give me an *O*. Oh, to heck with it! Go, Mukluks." And the basketball team—their shirts would have so many letters sewn on the front that the players would fall on their faces from all the extra weight.

"I haven't asked you this before," Daniel said, "but if you are right about going home, maybe this is my last chance. Do you know what will become of me?"

Walker hesitated. He had been trying to remember what did become of Daniel. He knew where he was buried, but he didn't know how he had died or why or when. He should have paid closer attention to the museum people during their talks. And it worried him that if he told Daniel what he did know, Daniel might do something different to avoid it. That might risk Walker's chance of going back to 2002. It might even prevent him from being born.

Finally, Walker said, "I didn't always listen closely to what the museum people said, but I know you are important in some group. The Masons, maybe. And I think you do something important for Stony Creek when Michigan becomes a state."

"And what happens to Stony Creek? What will it be like in your time?"

"It doesn't change a lot really," Walker said. "It becomes pretty much what your father wants—a small village with hardly any car traffic."

"Car traffic?" Daniel asked.

"Yeah, you know, cars," Walker said. "Cars, short for . . . motorcars, I guess. Automobiles, horseless carriages, buggies with engines." Walker couldn't imagine life in his time without cars being practically everywhere.

"Well, I'm confused by all this 'time' stuff," Daniel said.

"Me, too," Walker agreed. "Anyway, I don't expect to be here tomorrow morning, so I just want you to thank everyone for me. They're the nicest folks I've ever met. Plus, I've learned more since I've been here than in all my years of school. I'm not just talking about planting corn and building mills and all of that. I've found out a lot about myself and people and history, too."

"I will tell them," Daniel promised.

"But you can't say where I've gone," Walker said. "And you can't tell them anything about how I widened Main Street on Governor Cass's map." Walker sat up and looked at Daniel. "If you do, someone might change it back to sixty feet. If Main Street isn't kept at one hundred feet, Rochester might become a ghost town before I'm born. I don't know what would happen then."

"All right," Daniel agreed. There was a long pause when only the steady hum of crickets outside droned into the darkened loft. "I will miss you, Walker," Daniel said. "I do not understand everything you have told me about the future, but I bet nobody has ever had a friend like you, someone from another time."

"Same here," Walker said. "Sometimes I lie awake and can't believe what's going on. Stuff like this only happens in movies."

"Movies?" Daniel asked.

Walker thought for a moment and then rested his

head back on the hard pillow. "Yeah, movies," he sighed.

Daniel blew out the candle and in minutes the two were asleep.

When morning light crept into the log cabin, Daniel looked over at his friend's bed. Walker was still there.

Daniel touched his shoulder. Before Walker even opened his eyes he knew he was still in 1824. It came as sort of a relief. He was awake now and he began to wonder, what if I never get back? What if I never see my parents or friends again? What if my trip here is a one-way ticket? He saw Daniel's smiling face. I guess that wouldn't be the worst thing that could happen.

"You are still here," Daniel said happily.

"Yeah," Walker said with a sigh. "Actually, I'm kind of glad. Today I would be starting my final exams at school. Without studying for the past few weeks, I'd have flunked 'em for sure."

"I have no idea what you are talking about," Daniel said, still smiling, "but I am glad you are here. The potatoes have to be planted today. Eunice and I could not do it without you."

"How do you plant potatoes?" Walker asked, pulling his shirt on over his head.

Daniel shook his head. "I cannot believe that you have never planted potatoes, or corn, or turnips," he said. "What do you do for food in your time?" Daniel asked.

"My mom goes to the grocery store every week,"

Walker said. "She buys everything—frozen pizza, potato chips, bagels, yogurt, OJ, bread . . ."

"Bread?" Daniel interrupted. "You mean you eat something I have heard of? Does any of it taste as good as what my mother makes?"

"Sometimes," Walker said. "Actually, some of it is pretty good. It's also really fast to make. You can nuke it in a microwave, and it's ready in thirty seconds."

"And what is the good of that?" Daniel asked.

"Well, you can spend your time doing other things," Walker said with a shrug.

"Like what?" Daniel asked.

"Oh, I don't know. Lots of things. Watch TV, listen to CDs, play games on a PC, or just hang out."

"Does anyone in your time use complete words or talk in full sentences?" Daniel asked. "You seem to have shortcuts for everything."

"I'm sorry," Walker said. "It's just that things go so fast where I'm from. We can hardly say a word without someone butting in. It's as if we know we're going to get interrupted, so we try to say everything as fast as we can. You should see my dad at his drug store. He can't say *hi* to a customer without his phone ringing."

"Phone?" Daniel said. "I heard you trying to explain to my father what a phone was that first day you came here."

"Yeah, that was really weird," Walker said. "When I got here, I didn't believe that he was really Lemuel

Taylor. I thought he was some wacko cult freak who was about to torture me to death. Anyway, a telephone lets you talk to people anywhere in the world. The one at my dad's store has five lines. He can talk to five different doctors about five different people. He has a computer linked to one line so he can do six prescriptions at once."

"Computer?" Daniel asked. "What is a computer?"

"Oh, man," Walker said with a cringe. He thought for a moment. "It's like a real complicated gadget that lets you cipher a million things at the same time. You can do math, write papers, get information from the internet—all in less than a second."

Daniel gaped in awe at his friend. A smile slowly crept across his face. He realized he was being told a whopper of a fib. "These computers, do they plant potatoes?" he asked.

"No, nothing like that," Walker said with a laugh.

"Well, that is too bad. If they did," Daniel said, moving to the loft ladder, "we could get one, let it plant the potatoes, and we could fish."

"Or golf," Walker said, knowing that he was leading Daniel into some new territory.

"And what might golf be?" Daniel asked.

"It's a sport, kind of, where you go out on a pasture and hit a little ball with a club. Then you spend the rest of the afternoon looking for it. Some people use all their leisure time doing it. It's great fun."

"This is getting good," Daniel said. "And just what is leisure time?"

"It's free time," Walker said. "You know, like here when you . . . uh . . ." Walker suddenly realized that since being in 1824, he had never seen anybody not doing something that wasn't necessary for survival. "I don't know, it's just time when you're not doing something important."

"And when do people in your time plant their potatoes?" Daniel asked.

"We don't plant potatoes. Someone else does."

"Well, we don't have anyone else to do this," Daniel said, "so maybe we should spend some of this morning's leisure time planting potatoes. We have about an acre to get into the ground today. Besides, they might keep us alive this winter."

"Right," Walker said. "What do you suppose your mom has cooked for breakfast?"

"I don't know, but I am sure it will be as good as anything your telephones or computers could make."

Chapter 18

❧ *Planting* ❧

The two boys hurried down the ladder to the table. Daniel was right. Mrs. Taylor had made a breakfast that could not be had anywhere in 2002. It was dried field corn that she had soaked overnight and then fried with bacon drippings in an iron skillet. She scraped the crackling kernels from the hot pan and spooned them into Walker's bowl.

Walker stirred in some fresh cream to cool it into a thick porridge. Over that, he poured some of the dark honey that Daniel had collected from the bee tree. Walker tasted it with the tip of his tongue. It was wonderful, better than *Captain Crunch*.

"We will begin the sawmill today," Mr. Taylor said from his place across the table. "Nathaniel and Elisha have chosen a site upstream where the river should have enough power to turn a wheel. With a sawmill we can make boards for our new homes. They will be proper wood-framed houses, each with several bedrooms, a parlor, and a kitchen. We will have large glass windows in every room as we did in Aurelius."

Daniel winked at Walker before turning to Mr. Taylor. "We have some leisure time this morning that we thought we'd use to plant the potatoes," Daniel said. "But after that we could help with the mill if you need us."

"Not today," Mr. Taylor said, glancing first at Daniel and then at Walker. "Elisha and Peter are gathering materials to make the saw. Perhaps you can help them. Mr. Mack has ordered six chairs for his new house in Pontiac. Also, I will be making the wheels for Nathaniel's new buggy. I might ask you three to help me with that. But do not worry, by the time you get the potatoes planted, I am certain someone will have something for you to do," he said. He stood up, grabbed his straw hat, glanced again at Walker, and then hurried outside.

"I don't think I'll be much help to your father," Walker whispered to Daniel. "I don't know how to do any of the stuff he was talking about."

"Do not worry about that," Daniel said. "He says that learning is what being young is for."

"For an old guy, your father sure knows a lot," Walker said.

"Maybe that is how he got to be so old," Daniel said with a grin. "Let's get Eunice and the bucket of potato eyes and start planting before it gets too hot out in the field."

Walker and Daniel left the cabin and met Eunice as she was picking a bunch of wild flowers outside the door.

"Are you ready, Eunice?" Daniel called to his sister.

"I will be along soon," Eunice answered. "I will take these inside to Mother and meet you in the field."

The two boys walked from the cabin toward the creek. They crossed the narrow Indian trail into a flat, fertile patch of land.

As Walker and Daniel approached the field, Daniel caught sight of something moving in the woods on the other side of the stream. It withdrew quickly behind a wide beech tree. Daniel, trying to see what it was, tripped on a stump and almost spilled the pail of potato eyes.

Walker also saw it. "Daniel!" Walker said. "Something's behind that tree—a wolf or bear or something."

"Hold still," Daniel whispered, "I think it is an Indian. I will find out who it is." He began to walk toward the beech tree. "Who is there!" Daniel called out.

An Indian boy nearly Daniel's size and perhaps ten years old stepped from behind the tree. He wore only buckskin breeches from his waist down leaving his feet and chest bare. Two crow feathers were stuck in the top of his long shining black hair.

"It is me, Ca-cob," the Indian boy said.

"Ca-cob, what are you doing?" Daniel said trying to hide his relief that it was not Wa-se-gah.

"I am here to see the one you call Walker," Ca-cob said.

"That is me," Walker said, glancing warily at Daniel. "What do you want?"

"Our people have talked much about you," Ca-cob said. "My father is the shaman of our tribe—a great medicine man. He has told us that you have come from far away. Like the Anishnabeg, our ancient ancestors, he has seen you in his dreams. He says you swim like my brother, the otter, the totem of our tribe. My father says that your heart is strong but your medicine is weak. You will need the medicine of our brother, the otter, to help you with your task," Ca-cob said. "I have come to give you what I carry with me." Ca-cob lifted a leather pouch from around his neck. He removed a buckskin cord with many colored beads around it. A shrivelled brown lump dangled at the bottom. He held it out to Walker.

"What is it?" Walker asked as he took it in his hand.

"It is the paw of the otter," Ca-cob said.

Walker cringed as he recognized the pads and claws of the animal's foot.

"It is strong medicine. You must wear it while you are here," Ca-cob said.

"Oh, gee, uh, I don't think I'll need . . ." Walker stuttered as he stared in disgust at the grotesque offering.

"My friend doesn't have the words to thank you," Daniel said to Ca-cob as he put the otter paw amulet around Walker's neck. "He is not familiar with the ways of his Indian brothers." Daniel stood back and admired the ugly trinket now hanging from Walker's chest.

Seeing that Ca-cob was not leaving, Daniel asked, "Why else have you come?"

"I am learning to track game," Ca-cob said. "But if I am not able to sneak up on two pale-faced boys, how could I ever stalk the swift and timid deer?"

"I am just glad you are not Wa-se-gah," Daniel said.

"If I were Wa-se-gah, you could have heard me from across the forest," Ca-cob answered. "Wa-se-gah could not sneak up on a fallen tree. Why would you be afraid of Wa-se-gah?"

"He does not like the white man," Daniel said. "Most of the Indians here are friendly, but some, like Wa-se-gah, are not. My father says that Wa-se-gah does not honor the treaty that allows us to be here."

Walker stood at Daniel's shoulder. "But your father has title to it," Walker said. "He paid for it."

"Yes," Daniel agreed. "But some Indians do not believe in those treaties."

"Daniel is right," Ca-cob said, looking Walker in the eye. "My people still talk of the days before white man came. We do not have books to tell us the old stories. Instead we listen to our parents and grandparents who teach us the ways of our ancestors. They tell the ancient beliefs of the first people, the Anishnabeg. They believed that no one has the right to give or take land. The earth, like the sun, the moon, and the wind, belongs to everyone. It is our religion."

"Your religion?" Walker said.

"Yes," Ca-cob answered. "Our people believe in owning nothing except what we make ourselves—our bows and arrows, blankets, and clothes. White man's religion says that he is to control the earth, but the Anishnabeg believed that all his spirit brothers and sisters must share everything. So some of my people do not accept the white man's treaties that give land to one person to keep for himself."

"Well, they're going to have to," Walker said. "Our government bought it from them. My dad told me about the treaty the Indians signed so this area could be settled by American farmers."

"Some of my people believe that the treaties were made unfairly," Ca-cob said. "The white man used many tricks to make my people agree to them."

"Most of the Indians are real good about it," Daniel said to Walker. "But remember, only ten years ago in the War of 1812, these same Indians fought on the side of the British against the Americans. The battles were bloody. Many people died on both sides. Hatred between the Americans and the Indians ran very deep. When the war was over there was much reason to fear each other. Pioneers who had come here to farm worried that Indians would wipe out their homes and families. The Indians feared that American soldiers would attack the Indian villages and kill all their people."

"You know a lot about history," Walker said to

Daniel.

"This is not history, Walker," Daniel said. "I remember the Indian raids back in New York when I was a little boy. Even now we never know what might start another war. Ca-cob's and our languages and beliefs are so different that even acts done in peace may be taken the wrong way and lead to a fight. A fight can become a battle and a battle grows to a war. Things can get out of hand in a hurry."

Walker saw Eunice running from the cabin across the field toward them. Suddenly she stopped when she saw the bronze-skinned person standing near Daniel and Walker. When she recognized him to be her friend, Ca-cob, she ran to his side.

"We are friends, Ca-cob," Daniel said. "Your family has been good to my family. You helped us through the winter last year. I am glad that you have come to visit us, Ca-cob, but we must now plant our potatoes. You will come again?"

"Yes," Ca-cob said, "and next time I will warn you so that you will not be frightened of your brother."

"That would be good," Daniel said with a smile. "We have no need to stalk each other. There are plenty of deer in the forests for that."

"You will wear the medicine of our brother, the otter?" Ca-cob said to Walker.

"Oh yeah–uh, sure," Walker said, looking down at the talisman hanging from his chest.

"I will be sure that he keeps it with him always," Daniel said. "My friend is not good at speaking what is in his heart, but he knows what an honor it is to be called a brother to your people."

At that Ca-cob turned and disappeared into the woods.

"We must get these potatoes planted before it gets too hot," Eunice said.

"All right," Daniel said heaving a sigh of relief. "Here is how it is done, Walker." He took the shovel and turned the moist black earth.

Chapter 19

Lemuel's Decision

"See," Daniel said, holding the shovel. "Just drop one of these potato eyes five or six inches into the ground and cover it making a little mound. Then go ahead about two feet and do it again."

"It is not very hard, but it can become tiring," Eunice added, handing her brother another potato eye.

"And it must be done," Daniel said. "Everyone has to do his part. If we do not plant these potatoes now, when winter comes and people begin to starve because the potato crop was planted too late, we would know whose fault it was. And besides, I did not come all the way from New York to starve."

"Why did you come?" Walker asked.

"Excuse me?" Daniel said, straightening his back.

"Why'd you come to Michigan?"

"Because Pa said," Eunice cut in, looking at Walker in surprise. "Whatever Pa says, everyone does. Come on, stop jabbering. It is getting hot."

"I remember," Daniel said, ignoring his little sister. "It was about three, maybe four, years ago. It was on a Sabbath, right after church. Everyone was sitting in our living room in Aurelius. The men were saying that the crops that had been so good when they first moved to Aurelius were not so easy to grow anymore. They knew of other eastern farmers who had gone west by the river route to Ohio, Illinois, or Indiana. A few had taken the northern way across Lake Erie to Michigan Territory. All were doing well with their crops."

"And most of the Indians that had lived around here had moved on," Eunice added.

"We almost decided on Ohio," Daniel said. "Then Nate told Father that Ohio was already a state and that all the good farming land had been taken. He thought we should go to Michigan Territory."

"My brother Harry said that Michigan was nothing but swamp," Eunice put in. "He taught us a rhyme:

> Don't go to Michigan, the land of ills,
> The word means ague, fever, and chills."

"Then Lewis Cass, the governor of Michigan Territory, came to New York to get people to move here," Daniel said. "He put on meetings where he talked about how great this place was. He said Michigan would be good for a strong pioneer family. There was fertile land for farming, tall trees for building, fast streams to turn a mill wheel—it had everything. He had some fellow with him who played a guitar and sang a song. It had several verses, but the first one went:

Come all ye Yankee farmers who'd like to change your lot,

With spunk enough to travel beyond your native spot,

And leave behind the village where Ma and Pa do stay,

Come follow me and settle in Michigan-i-ay."

"He gave out the words on a broadsheet," Eunice said as she put another potato eye into the ground. "Pretty soon everyone was singing it."

"Mr. Cass told about how the Erie Canal was being built," Daniel said. "It wasn't finished yet, but parts of it were done. People could go on it for a ways and then take a wagon until they got to another part that was done. Eventually they would get to Buffalo. From there a big steamboat would take them across Lake Erie."

Walker worked with the shovel in front of Daniel and Eunice as they told him about that meeting back in New York.

"One of the men asked about crossing Lake Erie," Eunice said. "He heard it was more dangerous than the Atlantic on account of it was so shallow. Winds could blow a big schooner onto a sand bar and break it into pieces."

"Yes," Daniel said, "but Mr. Cass told how the government was building lighthouses to make sailing safer.

Also, a new steamboat called *Walk-in-the-Water*, could get across Lake Erie in any weather. It did, too, until it went aground in '21. They saved its engine and put it in a new ship called the *Superior*. That is what Elisha came across on two years ago. When he got here and saw this piece of land, he staked it out and bought 160 acres for $1.25 each with money Pa had sent him with."

"By the time Elisha got back to Aurelius," Eunice said, "it was too late for us to come out that fall. But Pa sold our land in New York for four dollars an acre which gave us a good start out here."

Walker, Daniel, and Eunice were close to the bottom of the pail of potato eyes when Daniel stood up and stretched his legs. "Pa said that with all sixty of us working together, our new town would be one of the biggest and best villages in all of Michigan Territory. Besides, Pa said that Aurelius was getting too crowded. All around him people were moving in and arguing about religious beliefs. That is what really got him when it came right down to it. Pa said he was just doing what his great- great-grandfather had done when he left England in 1635. It was high time for another move."

"So that is why we came," Eunice said as she plunked the last of the potato eyes into the ground.

Walker looked over the acre of land they had planted. Another job done, he thought. If I hadn't been here to help, would this crop have been sown? Was this the reason I was sent here? Will I go home now? Maybe. Probably not. Daniel and Eunice could have done this without me. Walker shook his head, not knowing what, if anything, was going to get him back to his place in time.

The gristmill would be done by the end of summer and ready for the fall harvest of corn and wheat. The sawmill was being built. The school house would be next. There didn't seem to be any end to the work, and Walker's help was vital to each project. Every day Walker became a more important part of Stony Creek, and Stony Creek became a more important part of Walker. This was his home now. Maybe for good.

Chapter 20

❧ *The Mill* ❧

" . . . And so, we gather for this, a most important day for the people of Stony Creek," Reverend Taylor proclaimed, standing before the door of the new gristmill. He faced the sixty people who had assembled by the river for the blessing of the mill. It was the last day of June, and the warm sun shone down upon them. "As pioneers in this wilderness we have built, with God's help, nine homes, a church, a blacksmith shop, and now this fine gristmill. It will supply us with flour and provide earnings from the grinding of other farmers' grain. I hereby dedicate this structure to God, for it is only by His grace that it was built. Let us bow our heads."

Walker stood near the back of the crowd, surrounded by his new family and friends. He lowered his head and clasped his hands in front of his chest. Everyone became still. Only the fluttering of leaves in a nearby poplar tree and the bubbling of the creek broke the prayerful silence. Walker slowly became aware that someone was murmuring behind him. Who could possibly interrupt Reverend Taylor's blessing? Walker wondered. Then he recognized the voices. It was Eunice and Daniel.

"I dare you," Eunice whispered.

Oh no, Walker thought. What is she up to now? He turned slightly, his hands still clasped in front of him. There were the two youngest Taylors standing nose to nose. Daniel was scowling at his sister, giving her the "don't-you-even-think-of-it" look.

"And now," Reverend Taylor continued, "we dedicate this building, as we have our lives, to God. Amen." There was a fervent amen from the rest of the onlookers. Walker knew each man, woman, and child by name. He knew what each did best to serve the community. He knew their faces. He knew their voices. He even knew their laughs. In the past month he had become one of them.

Walker looked at the mill. He had learned from Reverend Taylor that pride was a sin, but he couldn't help but be pleased at the part he had taken in building it. He had been there from that first day when he helped lift the millstone into place. He had nailed the boards to the frame. He had dug the millrace trench that would provide the power to turn the stone.

Not one bushel of corn had been ground but, Walker knew the milling process from top to bottom.

"Now," Reverend Taylor said, "Brother Millerd has some words to add to the dedication. Nathaniel, would you address the people?"

As Nate Millerd came through the crowd, Walker's thoughts began to stray. What could Eunice be daring

Daniel to do? he wondered as he stared at the new building. It was beautiful. Three stories tall, well-sided, the wheel rolling smoothly with the flow of the millrace water. His eyes were drawn to the eight-inch square hoisting beam that stuck out ten feet from a double door high in the loft. The beam would be used to pull sacks of grain up to the storage bins.

Walker stared at the wide, squared–off timber. It reminded him of the beam in the barn that Eunice had double-dared her brother to run along before jumping onto Daisy's back. What a foolish and dangerous ride that was! He turned to see if Daniel and Eunice were still arguing. They were not, but he did notice that Eunice had her eyes fixed on the mill's new hoisting beam high above the mill pond. In the next instant Walker knew what the two had been quarrelling over.

Walker quickly worked his way to the back of the crowd. He heard Daniel whisper to his little sister, "You are not going to do it. You are foolish to even think about it."

"I am not doing it," Eunice defended with a taunting smile. "I am daring you to do it."

"Not me! I am not walking that beam," Daniel said, shaking his head.

"Then I will double dare you," Eunice said with a huff.

Walker edged closer to the young Taylors as Nate asked everyone to bow their heads for his prayer.

"Dearest God in Heaven," Nathaniel began, but Walker wasn't listening. He was standing beside Daniel and Eunice.

"Neither one of you is going to do it," Walker said. "Dare or no dare. That's twenty feet straight down, and the water is fifteen feet deep!"

"I am so going to do it," Eunice said. "And you can't stop me."

"Look," Walker said calmly. "Suppose you fall into the pond. Can you swim to shore?"

"I will not have to," she said, her little nose pointing to the sky. "I will hold my breath and come right up to the top. The stream will carry me to one bank or the other, and I will simply crawl out. Then I can watch Daniel do his part of the double dare, and laugh when he falls in. Besides, I will not fall."

The rest of the Stony Creek people kept their heads bowed as Brother Millerd continued his prayer.

Eunice glanced at Nathaniel as though she had just then realized that a prayer was being given. She turned to Daniel and, pointing to Nate, gave Daniel a "hush" sign. She then struck an angelic pose, pretending to listen to Nathaniel's prayer. As soon as Daniel turned his head toward Nathaniel, Eunice slipped away. In the next instant, Daniel looked back and realized that he had been tricked. He saw Eunice's long hair flowing behind her as she darted around the crowd toward the mill.

Daniel raced to catch her, but by the time he got to the door Eunice was already running up the stairs. Nathaniel finished his prayer just as Daniel vanished into the mill behind him.

After the Stony Creek community said their amens and opened their eyes, they saw Eunice stepping from the loft door twenty feet above the pond onto the narrow beam. Daniel appeared in the doorway and reached for her. But he was too late to stop her. All he could do now was hold his breath.

"Look!" Peter Groesbeck yelled, pointing to the top of the mill.

"It is Eunice!" Sarah Millerd exclaimed.

"Eunice!" Lemuel Taylor hollered. "Come down from there at once!" But he might as well have called out to the moon.

With her arms outstretched for balance Eunice took her fourth step, now halfway to the end of the plank. She began to sway from side to side. The look in her eyes was no longer brazen and bold. Still, she moved forward.

"Please, Eunice," Walker yelled. "Turn around! Come back!"

Eunice glanced toward Walker and forced a smile. She took another step and as she did, her left heel caught the edge of the beam. Her nervous grin changed instantly to a look of terror. Her foot flew high over her head and she spun in midair. The next moment the back of her head slammed the hardwood beam with a crack that could be heard throughout the village.

Eunice's small, tense body went limp. She fell like a rag doll and splashed into the pond below. Quickly she drifted to the center where the pond was deepest. There the current began to send her in large circles. The air trapped in her petticoats escaped slowly as she went around in the whirlpool. Slowly she began to sink lower in the pond. Soon only her head remained out of water.

The crowd rushed to the water's edge. Walker struggled to push his way through the people. He heard Mrs. Taylor scream, "Help! Save her! She is drowning!"

Nathaniel Millerd yelled, "Someone, swim after her!"

At once Walker remembered Daniel telling him that no one in the village knew how to swim. It would be up to him to pull her out. By now she had already disappeared beneath the surface. Walker peered into the deep black pond. ""Where is she?" he shouted.

A voice from high above called to him, "There, Walker! Right there!" It was Daniel standing at the opening of the mill loft. He pointed to a place ten feet in front of Walker. "Look for her white dress!" he yelled.

Walker stared at the place where Daniel was pointing. "Yes! I see her!" Walker screamed. He reached for his shirt to tear it off, but his hand caught hold of the otter paw amulet that Ca-cob had given him. Walker glanced at it and remembered Ca-cob's strange message. "It is strong medicine. You must wear it while you are here." He took a deep breath and dove in head first.

Walker pulled at the water with his arms and scissor-kicked with his legs as he kept his eyes on Eunice's white clothing. His ears screamed in agony as he went deeper. He remembered his dive two weeks earlier when he tried to get a stone from the bottom of the pond. Even if he could grab hold of Eunice, would he be able to return to the surface before running out of air? He knew it was possible that he could drown with her.

Still, Walker pulled down through the cold water, kicking and stroking as hard as he could. The pressure in his ears and chest continued to build. Finally, she was before him, her face contorted in pain. Walker grabbed her waist and set his feet on the rocky bottom. He bent his knees and pushed off. His ears were bursting and his lungs felt as if they were being crushed between two millstones. Holding Eunice with his left hand, he pulled through the water with his right.

Walker fought the urge to breathe as he sliced upward. He had to inhale, but he knew that the breath he would take would be the cold, black water of death, not only for him, but for Eunice as well. His thoughts flashed back to his last day in 2002 when he almost drowned while fishing in exactly this part of the stream. He clenched his jaw and squeezed his eyes to fight the overwhelming urge to inhale. As he opened his eyes he saw bright sunlight filtering through the water.

In the next instant, Walker exploded through the

surface. He gulped a huge breath of air, and   pushed Eunice's face out of the water. A gasp of joy burst from the crowd, but it was tempered by the fear that Eunice might already be dead from cracking her skull on the beam or drowning.

Walker kicked toward shore. Lemuel Taylor jumped from the high bank into the shallow water. He reached for his youngest child and taking her in his arms, set her gently on the grassy shore. With a nimble leap he followed, quickly turning her onto her stomach. He began the same lifesaving procedure he had used to save Walker only a month before.

Walker stood in four feet of water, his chest heaving with each breath. He grabbed an overhanging tree branch to keep from being swept downstream. He needed rest before crawling up the high bank.

From the mill loft door Daniel had watched Walker's heroic dive. When he saw Walker surface with Eunice in his arms, he ran down the stairs to the river bank. "Here, Walker!" Daniel yelled as he fought through the crowd. "Grab this stick!"

Walker reached toward him with his right hand. Just then the branch Walker had been holding snapped. He stepped back to brace himself but the rock he put his foot on gave way in the shifting sand. Walker slipped backwards and fell into the deep, fast-moving water. The river current quickly pulled him away from Daniel.

In the distance, Walker heard a loud cough–and then

a chorus of cheers. "Hurray, she's alive!" the Stony Creek villagers yelled.

Walker tried again to reach the stick Daniel held out to him. "Help!" Walker yelled, but as he called out he was sucked under by a whirlpool. Cold black water filled his lungs.

The crowd ran to Daniel's side. They searched the swirling river but saw no sign of Walker.

Some people stood on the water's edge, murmuring in disbelief at how quickly he had vanished. Others ran downstream hoping Walker would surface in the shallower rapids. Still others ran upstream and crossed to the other side thinking they would see him from the far bank.

Lemuel Taylor cradled his daughter in his arms and hurried up the hill to the log cabin where Mrs. Taylor warmed her with soup, blankets, and dry clothes.

An hour passed. Then two. Daniel stood alone on the river bank, stick in hand, until the tears had dried into long, muddy streaks on each side of his face. He turned and strode slowly to the cabin. He joined his parents and gave his sister a kiss and a farewell hug for Walker.

For the others who searched until dark for the young hero who had saved the darling of their village, there was no celebration.

Chapter 21

Return

Walker stirred. He blinked and realized that he was stretched out on the ground, flat on his back. A man knelt beside him holding Walker's jaw open and blowing air into his mouth. The man looked up and yelled into the distance, "Jill! Hurry! Get Dr. White! I think he's upstairs."

Walker began to cough. He writhed in agony and tried to focus his eyes on the man. To his surprise, it wasn't one of his pioneer friends. Who could he be? Walker suddenly realized it was the guy who ran the museum! McVay or McKay or something. He had spoken to his history class just last month. It was someone from his own time!

Walker knew the museum director was always around when his dad did the Halloween ghost walks. Walker had thought that, for a guy who made his living doing such a dweeby thing like studying history, he was a fairly "with-it" sort of fellow. Walker tried to get to his feet, but nausea swept over him and he fell back to the ground.

"Steady there," the museum director said. He looked

away and called to a woman rushing toward them. "Good, Jill, toss me the blanket. Did you find him?"

"Yes, he's getting his bag. He'll be right here."

A dozen people raced down the hill, many of them wearing old-fashioned clothes. Others were dressed in modern attire—jeans, shorts, and tee-shirts. Walker glanced at each of the faces and tried to figure out for sure which time he was in. Except for the museum guy, none of the people looked familiar. He decided that, if it was 1824, he would know everyone. Since he didn't, he must be home.

Walker was overcome with joy that he had earned his way back from the past. All of the scheming he had done while he was with Governor Cass—the planting and shoveling and hammering while he was with his pioneer family—all of that had meant nothing. Clearly he had gone back in time from 2002 to 1824 for only one reason—to save one special little girl, his great-great-great-grandmother, Eunice Taylor.

As Walker took all of this in, he suddenly realized he would never see her again—nor would he ever be with Daniel, who he knew for a fact was dead and buried in the Stony Creek cemetery with all of Walker's other pioneer family and friends. Lemuel and Sarah Taylor's children, their grandchildren, and even their great-great-grandchildren were dead, too. But their great-great-great-grandchildren, Walker's dad, aunts, and uncles were alive and well and thriving in the community Walker had helped to build 178 years earlier.

A warm blanket covered Walker from his chest to his toes. It felt just like the one Mrs. Taylor had put over him when he first arrived in 1824 over a month ago. Soon, Walker heard more people coming down the hill.

"My bag, please," Dr. White said. A black satchel came from the crowd. The doctor snapped it open and removed a stethoscope.

Walker felt a cold metal disc on his chest.

"We must keep you conscious," the doctor said. "Breathe deeply, son. What is your name?"

"Walker," Walker whispered. He coughed again and then croaked, "Morrison. Walker Morrison."

"Your dad owns the drug store?" Dr. White asked.

Walker nodded.

"I'm going to ask you a few questions, Walker," the doctor said as he probed the side of Walker's neck. "I need to find out if you hurt your head, okay?"

"Okay," Walker said.

"How many fingers do you see?"

Walker opened his eyes. Everything was a blur. He blinked. The hand came into focus. "Four," he said.

"Good. How old are you?"

"Thirteen," Walker said before going into another coughing fit.

When it stopped, the doctor asked, "Where do you live?"

"Rochester. Fourth and Walnut."

"What state?"

"Michigan Ter. . . uh, Michigan," Walker said. nearly adding "Territory," before he caught himself.

"And what is today's date?" Dr. White asked. He thumped Walker's chest with the tips of his fingers.

"June," Walker paused. "The 30th, I think. I'm not sure."

Dr. White leaned back with a puzzled look. He reached into his bag and brought out another piece of equipment. He clicked a switch and pointed a beam of light into Walker's eyes. "What year?" he asked.

Walker hesitated. He looked at the faces and clothes of all the people who surrounded him. "Twenty-oh-two," he finally said.

"Fine," Dr. White said. "Can you sit up?"

Walker nodded. He took the doctor's hand and pulled himself to a sitting position. His chest muscles ached as if they had been ripped from his ribs. He coughed hard and winced in pain.

"That's good. You need to get everything out of your lungs," Dr. White said. He listened once again with his stethoscope as he tapped Walker's back. "I'd like you to try to stand now." The doctor looked at the museum director. "Give me a hand here, Pat. He might be a bit shaky."

Walker got to his feet grabbing the physician's arm with one hand and leaning on the museum director's shoulder with the other.

"I want you to come to the farmhouse with Mr. McKay and me," Doctor White said. "Don't be afraid, son. You are going to be fine. I'll call your parents. They will come and take you home soon."

"But my bike," Walker said, "I left it over there last month when I got here." Walker pointed to the bridge.

"Last month?" the doctor said.

"Yeah," Walker replied. "It's still there. I can see it."

"Mr. McKay will keep it here for you. You can pick it up later," Dr. White said. "I don't want you riding until we're sure you're okay. I'll stop by your house tonight after my rounds."

Walker suddenly thought about Renee St. Jean. He glanced toward her patio. Her house was there, but she wasn't. School had been over for several weeks, so she was probably with her parents at their chalet in the Loire Valley. Had Kenny taken her to the last dance? That would be the first thing Walker would do when he got home—call Kenny and ask him about her. It suddenly occurred to him that, since he had been missing for over a month, everyone would think he was dead. I'll bet they had a funeral for me and everything. Just like in Tom Sawyer.

He turned and held the arms of Dr. White and Mr. McKay. The three hiked up the hill to the back door of the farmhouse. Mr. McKay ushered Walker into the kitchen where the aroma of fresh rhubarb pie drifted in from the window sill. The two men sat Walker down on a bench in the breakfast nook. They then moved down a short hallway toward the front door.

Walker could hear them speaking in hushed tones as they stood in the vestibule. "I wonder where that June 30th thing came from," Walker heard Dr. White say. "I checked him over from head to toe and found no concussion or internal injuries. The cold water may have affected his reasoning, but other than that he seems perfectly normal. I'll tell you this, I've never seen a drowning victim recover so quickly. You must have been right there when it happened, Pat."

Walker heard Mr. McKay suggest that they go outside. The front door opened, and that was the last Walker heard of their conversation.

"Not really," Mr. McKay said as the door closed. "It wasn't like he was swimming toward me when I first saw him. I just happened to be walking along the creek trying to collect my thoughts about something else. That's a long story, too."

"You don't normally go down there?" Dr. White asked.

"Not often. But anyway, that's where I was," the museum director said. "As I walked along the creek I glanced down and noticed a Detroit Tigers baseball cap floating on the water. It was hardly wet. Then I saw a fly rod drift by. I jumped from the bank into the shallow water and grabbed the hat and pole. I tossed them on shore and was about to climb up when my eye was drawn to something very deep, maybe ten or fifteen feet under water. It looked like a department store dummy like you see at Mitzelfeld's. It was swirling up, face down, from the bottom."

Dr. White opened his black case and returned the stethoscope he had been wearing around his neck.

"It didn't float up really," Mr. McKay continued. "It was more as if it were being drawn to the surface by some unseen current, an invisible force. It was lifeless, stiff as a board, and came right to my feet. I grabbed it by the shirt and pants and pulled it ashore. I knew immediately that it was a person. I started mouth-to-mouth right away. Between breaths, I yelled up to the farmhouse for help. The rest you know."

"What do you make of his clothes?" the doctor asked.

"Yes, that is strange," Mr. McKay said. "He's dressed like one of our historic re-enactors. They come here for special events during certain holidays—Memorial Day, Heritage Festival, the Fourth of July, Halloween. But nothing is going on right now. The employees here at the museum wear period costumes for the visitors every day, but other than that . . ." Mr. McKay shrugged. "I can't explain it. Not yet, at least. I'll ask him about it, you can be sure of that."

"I have to run," the doctor said. "Afternoon rounds at the hospital, you know. I'll call his dad from my car phone. I know the store's number. I'm certain one of his parents will be here soon. Remind them to keep him sitting up, moving around, and awake until I see him at his house."

"Okay, Doctor," Mr. McKay said. He shook his head and stared absently into the distance.

"What's the matter," Dr. White asked.

"So much about this is strange," Mr. McKay said. "The water in the stream for one thing. It is not that deep. When the mill was working 150 years ago there was a mill pond here, but not anymore. It's only three feet now at the deepest. Perhaps my eyes were playing tricks on me," the museum director said. "For another thing, I don't understand how he recovered so quickly."

"I don't either," Dr. White said, "but if I tried to figure out all the miracles I've seen in my life, I wouldn't have time to watch for new ones. I just chalk them up to divine intervention and let it go at that. I'll see you later, Pat."

Walker heard the screen door open and slap shut. He noticed a puzzled look on Mr. McKay's face as he returned to the kitchen. The museum director went to the window ledge, cut two slabs of pie, and poured two glasses of milk from the old GE ice box. He brought them to the table and sat down across from Walker.

Walker glanced around the room at all the modern inventions, the telephone, the light bulbs, the gas stove. Man, how we could have used those things in the 1820s, Walker thought.

Pat McKay stared into Walker's eyes with the expression of someone who was just about to solve a great mystery.

Chapter 22

☙ *The Letter* ☙

"Walker," Pat McKay spoke softly, "I would like you to tell me what happened—right from the beginning—everything that you can think of since you came here to fish."

Walker looked down at the pie as he thought about what he should say. *If I tell him that over a month ago I was suddenly thrown 178 years into the past—and now I have returned—he'd never believe me, no more than the Taylors would have bought my story that I had just dropped into their village from 2002. Still, if I can make anyone believe me, it will be this history guy who knows more about Stony Creek than anyone in the world. When I tell him what I know about all the people I met, he'll have to believe me.*

Walker cut the pie with his fork. He put the bite into his mouth, chewed slowly, then swallowed, all the while staring at the anxious face of the museum director before him. He knew that Mr. McKay had spoken to him about being related to the Taylors in Mr. Dillon's history class, but that was over a month ago. Mr. McKay obviously did not remember it or he would have said something. Instead, the museum director simply looked geekishly excited as if awaiting some shred of historic wisdom Walker might provide. Yes, Walker thought, if I can convince anyone, it will be Mr. McKay.

"This is going to sound nuts," Walker began, "but last month I came here after school to do a little fly-fishing. It was, maybe, the twentieth of May. I'm not sure of the date, but it was a Friday. I remember that."

"Sunny day?" Mr. McKay said, "sort of like this?"

Walker glanced outside through the small wavy panes of the old kitchen windows. "Yeah, pretty much, I guess," Walker said. For the next ten minutes Walker described the weird fish he'd hooked, how he had gotten trapped by the branches of the fallen tree, and how he had been forced underwater by the current. "The next thing I knew, I was on the river bank being rescued by Lemuel Taylor."

"What makes you think it was Lemuel Taylor?" Mr. McKay asked.

"He told me," Walker said simply. "Besides, after he saved me, I lived with his family for over a month. I ate with him, went into Rochester with him, built a mill and worked with him—it was Lemuel Taylor, all right. I stayed in his loft with his son Daniel. We got to be good friends, Daniel and me. Daniel is a great guy. He knows all sorts of stuff about fishing and finding honey and things you'd never believe a kid would know."

"Okay," Mr. McKay said. "After the man saved you,

what happened?"

"I walked with him and Mrs. Taylor to their log cabin. It was right over there," he said pointing to the orange plastic fence sixty feet away where people had been excavating the ruins of the Taylor log cabin for years.

Walker told Mr. McKay about how his regular clothes and shoes were torn to shreds in the stream and that Mrs. Taylor borrowed some from Nate Millerd—except for shoes which, since nobody had feet as big as his, he hadn't worn for over a month. Then he told about how he helped build the gristmill, planted potatoes, and fished for grayling. He showed Mr. McKay the otter paw that Ca-cob had given him. Finally, he got to the part about how Eunice double-dared Daniel to walk the beam on the new mill. He told how she had gone out on the plank and fallen into the pond. He explained how he dove in and pulled her from the bottom of the whirlpool and how Daniel had reached for him with a stick.

"I fell backwards, got sucked under, and the next thing I knew, you were pumping air into me," Walker said. He stopped and poked another forkful of pie into his mouth. "That's most of it."

Mr. McKay stared. "Is there anything else?"

Walker thought for a moment. There was an odd tone to Mr. McKay's voice that was beginning to make Walker uncomfortable. "Sure, there were lots of little things," he said. "I met Governor Cass, John Hersey—you know—stuff like that.

" Say, I heard you talking to Dr. White before he left. He seemed to wonder about that date I told him down there at the creek. I could be wrong about this being June 30th. It's around there, right? Twenty-ninth, maybe? July first? I've kind of lost track. That's not a big deal, is it?"

Pat McKay eyed the boy in front of him. Finally he said, "Walker, I want you to listen to me carefully. First, look behind you. Do you see that calendar?"

Walker turned his head and noticed a North Oakland Community Bank calendar hanging on the wall behind him. It was set to the month of May, 2002. Walker nodded.

"Do you see all those *X*s through the dates?" Mr. McKay asked.

Again Walker nodded.

"What is the last *X* you see?" Mr. McKay said.

"May 20th," Walker said, shrugging his shoulders. "Must be your *X* marker is on vacation, eh?"

"No one is on vacation," Mr. McKay said slowly. "Walker, do you recognize me?"

"Sure," Walker said. "You spoke to our Michigan history class last month. I thought you didn't remember me since it was so long ago, and I was sitting at the back of the room. What of it?"

"What of it, Walker, is that today is Friday, May 20th." He nodded his head toward an electric clock that hung on the wall a few feet from the calendar. "It's 4:20 in the afternoon. Hart Middle let out a little over an hour ago. I asked you about your family's relationship to the Taylors just as the last class of the day was ending. I saw you leave the school on your bike as I was getting in my car. With your ride from school to your house in town and out here to Stony Creek, you couldn't have been on the stream for more than five minutes before I found you."

The significance of Mr. McKay's words struck Walker like a cannon ball. His jaw dropped, his head snapped back, and his eyes popped wide open. "What?" Walker gasped. "That's impossible!"

"Well, it's true, Walker," Pat McKay said. "Look, I don't believe in time-travel. Yes, I know that it's fun to think about, you know, going back and forth through the centuries as easily as pedaling up to Lake Orion and back on our bikes, but it just can't happen. Besides, the very thought of it makes me wonder about all the things I would change if I could travel through time—the things I'd collect, the events I could witness, the people I could talk to while they were alive . . ."

Walker sat there, shaking his head.

Mr. McKay stood up and went to his office in the next room. He opened a large roll-top desk, picked up an envelope, and brought it to the kitchen table where Walker was sitting.

Mr. McKay sat down and began to speak very slowly.

"All the things you've told me, Walker, you could have had flash through your mind in a split-second, like they say about dreams. Did you know that scientists think that even those long dreams that we have during the night really happen in just a few seconds?"

Walker shook his head. He'd never heard of such a thing.

"Our brain works so fast that we are able to create fantastic adventures almost instantly—tales that might take hours or even days for us to plot if we were awake."

"What are you getting at?" Walker said.

Mr. McKay continued, "All the things that you told me—planting the potatoes, building the mill, catching the fish—all those things could have been stories you heard while you were following the re-enactors during one of your Halloween visits. Those are all stories that are told by some very convincing people, including your father. I know you've been here several times for those programs, right?"

"Sure, but this is different," Walker said angrily. "You don't believe me! I knew I shouldn't have told you. But it happened. It was no dream!"

"I know it could seem that way," Mr. McKay stood again and said in a calming voice. He put his hand on Walker's shoulder as Walker began to rise from his seat.

"Okay, what about these clothes?" Walker argued. He twisted away from Mr. McKay's grasp and stood taller by a head than the man in front of him. "Tell me how I got these clothes if I didn't get them like I said."

"You could have borrowed them from your father," the museum director replied. "Your dad wears outfits like this when he portrays Lemuel Taylor."

"But I didn't!" Walker said. "Mrs. Taylor gave them to me. They're Nate Millerd's. You've got to believe me."

Mr. McKay was silent for a moment. He sighed and leaned back in his chair. "In fact, I do," Mr. McKay said.

Walker stared blankly at the museum director. He was shaken by the sudden change in Mr. McKay's attitude. "You do?" Walker said. "I don't understand. Why the big turnaround?"

"Please sit down, Walker," Mr. McKay said. "I have much to tell you."

Slowly Walker returned to his seat.

"I believed you all along, Walker, but yours is such an extraordinary event that someone my age cannot accept it without question. I needed you to convince me—and you have—but there is more than what you have said that has made me believe."

Mr. McKay took the flat manila package from the seat beside him. He opened it and slid a faded envelope onto the table. From that he removed two handwritten pages. "This came in the morning mail," Mr. McKay said.

He showed Walker a rubber-stamped message on the front that read, NO KNOWN ADDRESS — RETURN TO SENDER.

"It had been sent to Pamela and Tiffany Howell in Aurelius, New York," Mr. McKay said, pointing to the center of the envelope, "but it apparently never reached its destination." Written in the upper left-hand corner was the return address, Eunice Taylor, Stony Creek, Michigan Terr. A blue one-cent stamp was on the right-hand corner. Walker recognized Eunice Taylor's hand-writing—big, looping letters, "t"s crossed in the middle, and "i"s dotted with tiny circles.

"Listen to this, Walker," Mr. McKay said:

Dear Pamela and Tiffany,

I am writing this to both of you because I wanted each of you to know about it. The strangest and most terrible thing happened yesterday. It started over a month ago when a new boy came here to Stony Creek. He was older than Daniel and me, but he was really dumb about everything. He was lost and had no place to stay. My mother and father said he could live with us until he found his family, so he roomed with Daniel in our loft.

Everything went well until yesterday during the dedication for our new gristmill. It was very bad of me, but I got it in my head to show off in front of all the boys in the village. I talked my brother into a double-dare, and, with everyone watching, I walked the hoisting beam on the new mill. I was halfway to the end when I slipped. I flipped backwards in the air and hurt myself real bad. When I woke up, my head ached something awful, and I was lying on the bank of the creek. My clothes were soaking wet and my father was pushing on my back.

Pretty soon my father carried me up to the cabin. Later on, Daniel came and told me that Walker Morrison, the boy who had come to stay with us, had dived to the bottom of the pond and pulled me out. When he tried to get himself out of the river, he fell and got sucked under. Everyone looked for him, but he never came up.

I feel awful. It was all my fault. I should never have gone out on that beam. But I feel worse because Walker had come to us like a lost boy, and in only a few weeks, he had become like a big brother to Daniel and me. He ate with us and everything. Daniel told me that after Walker saved me, he went to where he was supposed to be—where he came from in the first place.

Daniel said that the only reason Walker was here was to save me. But that makes no sense. How *could he know that before getting here? Then Daniel told me not to tell anyone, because no one would believe me. But I just have to tell someone, so I am telling you. That is everything I know, which I do not think is all there is, but Daniel said that if he told me everything, I would think he was crazy. So, all he would say is that Walker is just fine where he is, and that I should not fret about him.*

I think Daniel means that Walker is in Heaven. Anyway, Daniel told me that Walker was like a gift to us—to all the people of Stony Creek. He said that Walker could only be here for a while and that it was time for him to go back to where he came from. Oh, girls, I do not know how I can believe my own brother when he talks so strangely. But I guess I will have to, because he said he would speak no more of it.

"She signed it, 'Fondly, Eunice.'" The museum director folded the two pages and slid them back into the envelope.

Walker sat before Mr. McKay in stunned silence.

Pat McKay looked up from the letter to the boy in front of him. Walker was having trouble swallowing, as if his last bite of rhubarb pie had swelled up double in his throat.

The museum director took a magnifying glass from his shirt pocket and handed it to Walker. "Look carefully at the right-hand corner," he said.

Walker put the glass up to the envelope. "It's just an old stamp," he said, his voice trembling.

"No, I mean the cancellation date," Mr. McKay asked.

Walker looked again. "July 2, 1824," Walker whispered. He looked up at Mr. McKay. "You mean to tell me that after 178 years, this letter was just returned today from the post office?"

"Yes," Mr. McKay said. "It must have been in a dead letter file all of that time. Someone must have discovered it and sent it here to Stony Creek. The odds of it happening and you arriving on the same day are unbelievable."

Chapter 23

✍ *The Promise* ☞

"I can't explain time travel, Walker," Mr. McKay said. "It's part of every culture's legends from every corner of the world throughout history, but it's never been proven."

Walker took a long swig of milk from his glass.

"Many of the things you did while you were there in 1824," Mr. McKay said, "may have been important, almost certainly to the settlers, but also to you. The hardest to believe is that you saved your own great-great-great-grandmother. Frankly, Walker, I don't want to think too hard about that. One 'what if' leads to another and pretty soon, my head starts to spin. Questions like, what if you hadn't been there to save her? What if she had died? Logically, if she had died, she would not have had children. If she didn't have children, ultimately you could not have been born. If you had not been born, who would have saved her? Who would be sitting in front of me right now?'"

Walker looked at Mr. McKay with a knowing expression, as if he was perfectly aware of what the museum director was going through.

"Do you see what I mean?" Mr. McKay said. "I am not comfortable talking to, touching, and seeing things that do not—can not—exist. And that's just for starters. That's why I was down at the river. When I saw you in the classroom today, I didn't ask you about your relationship to the Taylors as an idle question. I had read Eunice's letter several hours before and was totally shocked when I saw your name on Mr. Dillon's roll. After school let out I came back here to the museum and went down to the stream to sort things out. From Eunice's letter I knew what was going to happen to you. I just didn't know how or when. As I was trying to decide if I should warn you—trying to figure out what would happen if I did and you didn't go back in time—you floated up to me from the bottom of the river. As soon as I turned you over and saw who it was, I was pretty sure it had already happened."

Walker took another bite of pie. He leaned back in his seat. "That's what I've had to do for over a month," Walker said. "Every moment of every day, as tired as I was at night, I couldn't keep from thinking how impossible it all was—how everything I did might change the future. It got so bad I finally gave up trying. I decided simply to live in their time and do whatever I could to help them, and myself, get through each day."

"I've been thinking," Mr. McKay said, "maybe you shouldn't tell anyone about this. We don't have any real solid proof, you know. All we have is some old clothes, a letter written by a little girl, and a dried-up animal foot. For me that's enough. But other people?" He shook his head leaving the question unanswered.

Walker wiped some crumbs from his upper lip with the back of his hand.

Mr. McKay continued. "Also, I'm afraid of what might happen to you if this gets out. Magazine and TV people will want you to tell your story in front of microphones, cameras—even lie detectors. All sorts of psychiatrists and paranormal investigators will hound you until one of them finds or makes up some little crack in your story. When they do, you will be attacked like a lamb in a cage of snarling wolves."

Walker listened carefully.

"Going back in time has never happened, except in fiction. But you're not fiction, Walker. You're real. Other real people–schoolmates, neighbors, even your own family—might think you dreamed all this up just to get some attention. They would never believe another thing you said for the rest of your life. On the other hand, I know that all of what you have said is true, plus a whole lot more you haven't told me yet."

Walker waved the loaded fork aimlessly in the air. At the mention of schoolmates, he thought of Renee. If no real time has passed, if this is still Friday, May 20th, Walker began planning, I will see her in class Monday. I can ask her to the dance, that is, if Kenny hasn't already. In fact, they may still be playing volleyball at

the park. If I hurry I could beat him to it. This isn't so bad after all. Besides, Mr. McKay is right. If I can hardly believe what has happened to me, why should anyone else? If I take this to the newspapers, any chance I have with Renee would be lost. She wouldn't want to be seen with someone who tells such wild stories.

"This may sound selfish," Mr. McKay said, "but what you know about Stony Creek would be of enormous help to me. I've been here for fifteen years. My staff and I have spent countless hours piecing bits of history together. Hundreds of volunteers have combed every cubic inch of dirt in and around that old cabin looking for clues that would us tell what life was like for the Taylors. Broken bits of plates and buttons have told us little of their day-to-day lives. But you were there. You stood with them in that cabin. You ate with them at their table. You worked with them as they built their mills, planted their crops, and struggled each day for survival. You could tell me more about the Taylors and this village in one hour than all of us have learned in all our years of research."

Walker's mind was only half on what Mr. McKay was saying. The other half was daydreaming about Renee. He could picture her cheek next to his with her arms wrapped around his waist slow-dancing to some old Beatles' song at next week's dance. All the guys—Kenny Fisher at the front—would be standing around gawking at him totally green with envy.

"You don't have to help us with this, Walker," Pat McKay continued. "I'm going to give you Eunice's letter. You may take it to the newspapers if you want, or you could put it away and keep it as a souvenir of your visit into the past. There's nothing in it that I'd be keeping from the rest of my staff that we don't already know, except the part about you. What do you say?"

Walker heard a car roll up in the gravel driveway. It had the unmistakable motor knock of his mom's old maroon and grey GMC van. The engine stopped and a door squeaked open. Walker heard footsteps. He took a deep breath and walked to the hallway. The front screen door opened and in rushed his mother.

"Mom!" Walker said, tears suddenly filling his eyes. He ran to her and held her as he had when he was a little boy.

"Walker! Are you okay?" She searched Mr. McKay's face for an explanation.

"He had a fishing accident," Mr. McKay said. "Luckily we got him out of the water quickly. Dr. White happened to be here. He examined Walker and said that he will be fine. He will come by your house tonight after his rounds to check on him."

Mrs. Morrison stepped back and looked at Walker. "Where did you get those clothes?" she asked. "And look at your fingernails! They're filthy! Walker, what have you been doing?"

"It's kind of a long story, Mom," Walker said. "I'll

tell you all about it when we get home."

"Here's the envelope, Walker," Mr. McKay said. He handed him Eunice Taylor's letter. "Take care of those clothes. They are very old, you know. Maybe you can wear them and become one of our re-enactors."

Jill walked in from the back door carrying a blue baseball cap. "I believe this is yours," she said.

"My Kirk Gibson hat!" Walker said. He looked at the underside of the bill. The signature of his favorite player wasn't even wet.

"I brought along your fly rod and bicycle, too," she said. "They're right outside."

Mrs. Morrison and Walker went through the front door to the car. He turned as he got to the van and looked back at the museum director standing by the farmhouse door.

"Thanks, Mr. McKay," Walker said. "Thanks for everything. I'll be back tomorrow after the store closes and I'll tell you everything I know. If it's all right with you, maybe I could take the part of Daniel Taylor in the next Halloween walk. I guess if anyone knows what he was like, it would be me."

PENGUIN HUMOUR

The Unabashed Alex Charles Peattie and Russell Taylor

Alex is the *Independent*'s daily strip-cartoon. With its characters drawn from every tax bracket – bullish Alex, bearish Clive, decidedly boorish Vince and their yuppie molls – and its lowdown on the downside of today's wealth generation, it chronicles the City's most exciting era ever.

Un Four-Pack de Franglais Miles Kington

Les quatre hilarious volumes de Franglais dans one mind-boggling livre! Avec cet omnibus vous pouvez relax avec le knowledge que vous won't be stuck for quelque chose à dire anywhere in the Franglais-speaking monde, et cope avec any situation, n'importe quoi, either side de la Manche, or even in it.

The Looney Spike Milligan

Would Mick Looney's father lie on his HP deathbed? Well, he had to lie somewhere. When he told Mick that they are the descendants of the Kings of Ireland, was he telling the truth? If he was, why is Mick mixing cement in the rain in Kilburn? 'Hysterical' – *Time Out*

How to Become Ridiculously Well-Read in One Evening
Edited by E. O. Parrott

This superbly efficient book allows one to savour the wealth of great literature without the time-consuming tedium of actually having to read it. Through these succinct encapsulations you will rapidly acquire almost everything worth knowing about 150 of the best-known books in the English language – and free your time to spend many more happy hours in the pub.

How to be a Brit George Mikes

This George Mikes omnibus contains *How to be an Alien*, *How to be Inimitable* and *How to be Decadent*, three volumes of invaluable research for those not lucky enough to have been born British and who would like to make up for this deficiency. Even the born-and-bred Brit can learn a thing or two from the insights George Mikes offers here.